SHADOW CAST

THE HAWTHORNE UNIVERSITY WITCH SERIES
BOOK 6

A.L. HAWKE

PHANTOM HEART, LLC

ISBN: 978-1-953919-94-6 (ebook)

ISBN: 978-1-953919-52-6 (paperback)

ISBN: 978-1-953919-49-6 (hardcover)

Library of Congress Control Number: 2024907017

This is a work of fiction. Witchcraft is included to infuse a sense of realism to the novel, but in no way is it supposed to represent actual practicing witchcraft, witches, or the religion of Wicca or Thelema. Any satanic groups portrayed in this series are purely fictional and not intended to represent actual people or organization(s). The book also includes fictitious names, characters, places, and incidents. Any public names are used solely for creative purposes. Any resemblance to actual people, living or dead, or to companies, institutions, or locales is entirely coincidental or accidental.

Line edited by Stephanie Marshall Ward

Proofread by Alexa B., alexabooks.wixsite.com/authors

Cover © 2024 by Brosedesignz

Published by Phantom Heart, LLC

27702 Crown Valley Pkwy D-4, #201

Ladera Ranch, CA 92694, USA

Printed and bound in the United States of America

First printing May, 2024

Learn more about A.L. Hawke at www.alhawke.com

Correspondence: contact@alhawke.com

1

GRIMA

I'M UPSTAIRS IN DARKNESS, WEARING A LONG FORMAL DRESS, standing before floor-to-ceiling windows in my bedroom. My face is for the gods. My hair is straight and perfect. I've got on dark mascara and black lipstick, but my gothic makeup is discreet. A yellow light shines below my feet. It's emanating from my outdoor patio, reflecting off the mist over the surrounding forest and the wild grassy field below. There are no stars out and the moon is occluded by clouds, but this view is so pretty. I think of all the things I love about Hawthorne—all our trees, our campus, Hilltop Bluff—the view from my bedroom is my absolute favorite. I know it was Alondra's favorite.

I hear laughter. Then the clash of dishes. Whatever's happening below, I think my boisterous BFF, Madison, is guffawing over something. Then I hear "Mrs. Wallace" followed by more guffaws. Okay, that's definitely Maddie, probably teasing me downstairs.

"Coming down, Cadence?" asks Bryce at the doorway. The bedroom brightens as he opens the door.

I turn and see my husband in his cute navy-blue button-down and black slacks. His short hair is perfectly combed. His face is clean-shaven. I shopped for those clothes when we went to downtown Atlanta a few months ago. He looks so professorly. I don't. My long, draping black dress will probably remind the kids downstairs of Morticia Addams. But that's really what's behind this secret meeting downstairs, you know. This isn't a special "honors" program at Hawthorne University, or even a party with faculty. It's a recruitment of witches for Hawthorne Forest.

"Sure, Bryce. I'm coming. I just needed to freshen up a bit more."

"You look great. I was afraid you left for a wandering."

"No," I say with a laugh. "Just...a little nervous, I guess. Not sure why."

"Alondra wanted this, Kate. She always believed in you. Anyway, Kenosha is already entertaining everybody."

"Kenosha's saving the day again?"

"Blessed be and let it be. Relaaax, everything is going to be fine."

Bryce reaches out a hand for me. I nod and tear my eyes away from our gorgeous outlook.

My dining room downstairs is completely transformed. All these kids look so formal. They're all girls. All genders are invited to the program, but only our special "ladies' club" has a special occult practicum, if you know what I mean.

The provost, Dr. Kenosha Trent, is yapping away in good spirits beside my very long oak dining room table. I'm so glad she looks stronger. She's in a suit with a curly wig, sitting in front of our gorgeous wall-sized window, looking out into the forest.

"Cadence," Kenosha says, standing up. "Dr. Wallace."

"Found her," Bryce says with a chuckle, before grabbing a napkin, sitting down, and draping it over his lap.

The whole table is totally decked out in this fancy-smancy

white tablecloth, covered in crystal glasses and real shiny silver. Alondra had some amazing stuff for guests. All the big dishes are in covered trays. Of course, somehow Kenosha finagled the school footing the bill. I couldn't afford it. I smell the delicious spices, potatoes, and roasted chicken underneath. My sister witches helped arrange the room before the guests arrived, but only a few are here. There are too many guests for my sisters to attend. Every place setting has red wine in a refined crystal glass shaped like a chalice, but most kids are underaged and are drinking soda. And there are tons of small lit candles on the table.

I sit at the head of the table, draping my white cloth napkin over my lap and scooting closer to the table. Maddie nods beside me with a reassuring grin.

"Welcome, guys," I say. "Many of you may be wondering why I invited you here to my house."

They're so focused. No...not just focused, nervous. I remember being freaked out when I first arrived at Alondra's antebellum mansion—now my house. Even Alondra herself was intimidating. Maybe I overdid the witchy makeup tonight too?

"Some of you were with us last year in my husband's metaphysical history class. Others just made it here to Hawthorne. Either way, I'm so excited about this new year and I look forward to meeting all of you. This special program seeks to go deeper into knowledge of magic and the occult. Many of you might have heard rumors. The program was renowned when Dr. Alondra Johansen used to teach. Well, we don't sacrifice babies or drink human blood, okay?" Some laugh nervously. "But things can get weird." I bite my lip. "Outside of class, we'll meet and talk about magic and try out some real rites. If you're averse to any of this, perhaps finding it against your religion or beliefs, then the program might not be—"

There's a loud thud against my front door. That's followed by incessant rapping.

"I'll see who it is," says Bryce.

"No, Bryce," Maddie says, pushing her chair back. "I'll go. Maybe it's your brother, Katie."

Damie? Hammering on the door?

"Umm...so, the reward for joining will be graduating with high marks from our university. But be warned: we'll be practicing real pagan rites. It might make you uncomfortable, so I encourage you to research what you're in for before you sign up. Talk to us."

There's another loud bang followed by a few rings of our doorbell.

"You all won't have to do anything you're not comfortable doing," Kenosha adds.

I get it. She's trying to relax them.

"Yeah," I say, "talk to the more experienced among us, like Josie and Jessica or Madison here. Or even Dr. Wallace. We don't bite."

"You fucking worthless witch! Step aside! I'm not here for a weak magus! I need Windstorm! Where's Windstorm? Where's the Hawthorne Witch!"

What the hell? That voice makes me feel grima. Do you know what grima is? It's that awful creepy feeling you get when you run your fingernails across a blackboard. Cordelia is grima.

"Cadence!" cries Maddie. "Cadence, you might want to come here and—"

"She's there?" cries Cordelia.

"She's in a meeting."

"What meeting? Are you conjuring inside now?"

"Why do you care, Adder? Why not come back another time? *Hey, wait a minute! No! No, no, don't go in there now!*"

Kenosha loses her smile. She quickly throws her white

napkin on the white tablecloth and scoots back her chair. So does Bryce. I rush with them into the hallway.

Cordelia, this large broad-shouldered, black-ink-tattoo-faced bitch that hung a psychotic friend from my patio once (well, we were never sure it was her, but I'm almost positive) is storming toward us. She looks ready to pummel me. She's so big, she's large enough to suffocate me just by sitting on me. Right now she's wearing a bright scarlet cloak. With the red cloak and black-tattooed face, she looks barbarous. I imagine all those scared girls' faces in my dining room. We can't let them see her.

I block the hallway before she gets closer to the dining room.

"What's this about?" Kenosha demands. "We're in a meeting, Adder."

"Ask her," Cordelia says, gesturing to me. "She's been casting. She knows damn well what it's all about."

"What are you talking about?" I ask.

"You've been casting," Cordelia says with a wicked grin. She looks down on me, as she's about a head taller. "Invoking Alu-s. My sisters have been haunted in their sleep for weeks. Panthera is about ready to go on the offensive, but my circle is afraid of you. I'm not scared of you. It would be my pleasure to go to war with your coven again."

"Why not come back and talk about this later?" asks Bryce.

"Shut up, High Priest. You're as weak as Blackbird."

"Bryce is right," Kenosha says. "If there's something going on with your circle, Adder, let's talk later. Not in front of my students."

"Glad to see you're feeling better," Cordelia says with a smirk, "after this wicked witch nearly killed you. Windstorm hurt you real good, so I hear?"

"I don't know what you're talking about, Cordelia," I snap. "I haven't cast any magic spells against you or your coven!"

"Cadence, keep your voice down," Kenosha warns.

"Last time you guys accused us," snaps Maddie, "it was Enora."

"The nightmares are coming from somewhere," Cordelia replies, shaking her head hard. "We know Katie was cursed before, but our oungan was killed by my master. There's not a whole lot of witches with this power left around here. Could be Samhain, but she wasn't taught dream casting. Cadence was. Unless it's your spell, Willow?"

"Get out of my house!" I shout. *"Get the fuck out! Why the hell did you let her inside, Maddie?"*

"Bitch barged in," Maddie says, shrugging.

"Threatening me, now?" Cordelia asks, looking down on me. "I know I'm on your hallowed ground. I don't care. I told you, I'm not scared of you." She sticks a finger in my chest. "I warn you. As grateful as master's been for your help in Alabama, she's ready for another fight. She wanted me to tell you that we don't cast shield spells. If the dreams don't stop, we're going to fight, and I promise you, witches, we'll bring more than just bad dreams." She looks up and then turns back toward the foyer. "Maybe we'll burn *this* house down this time."

Before I hurl her across the room, she lifts her palm with a black tattoo of a backward pentacle. Then she quickly gathers her long red cloak, turns her back on me, and storms out the front door.

The door slams shut.

"Cadence?" Kenosha turns to me, suspicious. "What's this about?"

I quickly shake my head. "I don't know."

"Shit," Maddie says. "I really hate that snake."

"Well," Kenosha says, nodding. She heaves a sigh. "Now we have to explain *spell casting* and *curses* to your guests, Cadence."

"You never know, Dr. Trent," Maddie quips with a nervous

laugh. "Maybe all the excitement will really help with the recruitment?"

2

CLASS

I'M WITH TWELVE STUDENTS SITTING IN A CIRCLE. NO, THIS IS NOT my coven. All of us are sitting along a large table in a classroom trailer on the edge of campus. It's a special graduate history class I enrolled in for fall, being taught by the most fabulous professor of all time, Dr. Stoferson. Dr. Stoferson is this frail, gray-haired old man who walks crouched, with a cane, and seems to have difficulty just opening his mouth. But, oh, what comes from those lips. it's like what the Hindus call "Gita"; you know, *Gita* means "song." Everyone always sits patiently around the table for the man to "sing his song" and share his pearls of wisdom. And not only is everything the guy says like a window into a library, he says it in such an insightful way.

I'm ignoring him. Look, I've got too much on my mind. Remember Cordelia? Enora is the most powerful witch I've ever known, and being on her most wanted list tells you why these pearls being taught about Louis the Fourteenth are just not holding my attention at the moment.

"If you ever get a chance to travel to Paris," says Dr. Stoferson very slowly, "come visit the palace in Versailles. The golden gates and walls are simply magnificent. When I went there, it was the first thing I did, and I loved it. Of course, the smells have changed a lot since the seventeenth century. It smelled far worse back in those Louis the Fourteenth days."

What the hell am I supposed to do with a murderous madwoman after me and my coven?

"Word is that back in those days, there was a limited number of toilets, so people relieved themselves behind curtains. Now it smells nice. If you get the chance to visit—"

Maddie suggested I call Liam. She's guessing Melanie could be up to her tricks again. Speaking of smelly, Melanie is this stinky witch so disgusting that the witch council refers to her as "Mud." Enora and I tried to forget our differences and team up to fight her last summer. Remember? Anyway, Liam fought Melanie once too, but he's a powerful warlock who doesn't want to practice magic anymore, so I'm not so sure calling him—

"Ms. Wallace," he asks, turning to me. "What would be the consequences at the time of such bad hygiene? Can you expound on some of the illnesses that would have been common in Versailles back in the Sun King's time?"

"Huh?" What's this really nice guy talking about? "What, Dr. Stoferson?" Oh, yeah, Versailles. But...what does he want to know?

"Can you expound on the types of illnesses that were caused by bad hygiene at the time of seventeenth-century Versailles, France?" Then he chuckles. "I joke of smell but it's important to understand why gutters and underground sewage were developed in our modern age. At the time, people did not bathe often because standing water was viewed as unhygienic."

He waits. Then he furrows his brow.

"Plague, Cadence," he says, nodding his head. "Plague."

"Cadence," snaps a voice by the front door of the trailer. "Psst, hey, Cadence. Come here." The door's cracked open, and I recognize the dark goth makeup and black clothes of one of my witches. It's Mira! I haven't seen Mira in months. She lives all the way in Florida. I see her skinny partner, Courtney, with her long blond hair but the same witchy black lipstick and eyeliner. She's waving at me too. Mira's gesturing with her index finger for me to go outside. "Psst, Cadence, come on. Come over here for a sec."

"Excuse me," I say, pushing out my chair. Everybody's staring at me. I grab my notepad and pen and stuff them in my leather bag. "Sorry, excuse me, Dr. Stoferson."

He lifts his eyebrow and then turns to another student. I think that's as mad as he ever gets.

"What about you, Ms. Pofrie?" he asks. "What do you think—"

"Hey, Mira," I say with a forced whisper, quickly guiding her by the elbow down the steps from the trailer classroom. Then I hug her and Courtney. "Hey guys. It's so great to see you! How long are you going to be in town?"

"Three years," Mira says. "I'm a graduate student at Hawthorne now, Cadence. Figured I'd stop popping up and just stay here. It was getting boring in Florida anyway. Things are always more fun around you."

"That's great!"

"Yeah. Kenosha, along with my grades, helped. Courtney's working out getting a teaching job at Flintwood High, Maddie's school."

"Thanks to Maddie, Meer," Courtney interjects.

"Yeah. Thanks to her. That's what stopped us from moving this past summer. It was all held up on account of Courtney not having a job. Maddie helped. Now we're just homeless."

"You can stay at my house."

"Bryce already beat you to it. Hey, was that good ole Dr. Stoferson in there? What was he talking about?"

"Shit."

"For real? I always liked him."

I guide them a little farther from class, down a walkway

shaded by more trees. After heading down a grassy hill for another minute or so, we're near our library, but the thicket is so dense here that all we see are the trees and the path.

"No, we were actually discussing shit in the seventeenth century. You should have taken his class if you're in the graduate program now."

"I tried," Mira replies. "You know I came pretty late and his classes are packed. Listen, from what I heard about Cordelia, Cadence, I believe Enora is certain you're attacking them. Cordelia took a huge risk showing up at your doorstep, on your hallowed ground. They really believe you're after them."

"Couldn't it be Melanie?"

"The council is unsure."

"I'm so tired of these mysteries, Mira," I say, heaving a sigh. "I didn't do anything to her. If anything, I hate Enora less than before. I even tried to call her and talk to her about all of this, but she's not answering her phone. She's apparently super pissed over something I didn't do."

"Better find out soon, Cadence. When Enora is angry, it doesn't take long for her to strike. Kenosha and I are planning to talk about it with the group this Friday, on the Sabbath. Kenosha's still convinced, along with some members of the council, that the spirit inside you is not good. I know you think it's Alondra. I think it's Alondra too, but... Kenosha still thinks it could be the demon Ekimmu. Then again, of course, even if it is Alondra acting inside you, she'd have a motive for haunting Enora after what Enora did to her."

"But Alondra told me to *save* Enora. She wouldn't have said that if she wanted to hurt her."

"But she's not really hurting her, when you think of it. She's pestering her."

"Whatever the hell's going on, I want Alondra out of me, however it can be done. I've wanted this for a year now."

Mira nods pensively.

"Meer wants to try a séance, Cadence," Courtney says. "She wants to contact the spirits inside of you and exorcise them that way."

"Yeah, let's meet with the group Friday and talk about it," Mira says with a nod. "Okay, Katie?"

"All right, Mira."

"Yeah. Listen, there's something else. Since Courtney and I are back in town now, we'd like to join the coven. I hear you're in need of new recruits anyway."

"You'll always be a Hawthorne witch, Mira."

"Told you, Meer."

"Yeah, well, she didn't say *you're* in, Courtney," remarks Mira with a smirk.

"You sure you want her back in your circle, Cadence?" asks Courtney, looking pissed.

I laugh.

3
____

ARCANA

I'M STUDYING IN THE LIBRARY. I WAS NEARLY EXPELLED LAST YEAR by Dr. Bainer, remember? Yeah, well, that professor hated me so much he tried to throw me out of our history graduate program, and if Kenosha hadn't intervened, I would have been expelled. So...I'm studying.

What am I studying? Eliphas Levi. *Transcendental Magic,* by Eliphas Levi. Eliphas was that guy who drew the Baphomet in the late nineteenth century. See the picture on the second page of the book? Alondra used to love to flash this drawing during class with a nice devilish scarlet background. You know, it's the famous depiction of a hermaphrodite with a goat head, two snakes making a caduceus—or his/her pervert penis—a pentagram, and two horns on the devil's head. It was used a century later in the Satanic Church by Anton Lavey to represent Satan. If you look closely enough, you see a bright moon and a dark moon showing the law of dichotomies in Hermetic magic. Dichotomies are so important in ancient magic. That same dichotomy is seen in the figure's fingers. One finger is pointed up, the other down. It represents the first sentence of the Emerald Tablet, an ancient tablet venerated by occultists. It means "as above, so below." In other words, what lies in the outside world resides in ourselves. So, you know, to an occultist, this is not just a pervert goat sketch. It's super deep stuff.

There's a large window to my left. A few stories below, a cement walkway is illuminated by a yellow glow from the tall streetlamps. The walkway is surrounded by trees and meanders into the woods. Farther out, I can just make out a larger central path between large brick buildings. Usually students are walking under all these yellow lights. Not tonight. School just started, and it's pretty empty around the library.

Do you remember when Bryce and I met at this same spot for our first "date?" Yeah, that's such a nice memory...

I look down at my open bag and see my old leather-bound book, *Broomstick*, by a Geography and European Civilization textbook. I bite my lip. I wonder what Alondra says on the subject of Eliphas Levi? I'm guessing, quite a lot. She was pretty fond of good ole Eliphas Levi and Crowley. So I reach down and pick up my Book of Shadows.

The thing about *Broomstick* is that it sort of has a life of its own. Sometimes you can read it like a regular book and recall which pages to flip to. Other times you have to *will* pages to appear... I bite my lip again, looking around the study room. It's all empty tables and chairs along windows and a few vacant lounge chairs beside couches. During dead week, it's packed. Not now. There's only one student studying tonight—a young girl, in a red Hawthorne sweater and wearing glasses, on the other side of the large hall. I close my eyes, move closer to my book, and hold my palm over the pages. I think of Levi, Baphomet, and Alondra.

Revelare, revelare, revelare, Alondra Johansen. Venite foras, magistra.

The pages fly open. I quickly open my eyes and glance at the girl across the hall. She's not taking any notice.

Words on an old stained blank page are quickly scratched

in Alondra's handwriting. As I read, I not only discern her writing, I hear her voice:

TWO PILLARS: GENDER

Ask why is there female, why is there male? There is no female without male. Ask why is there Michael, why is there Samael? There is no angel without the devil. Why is there heaven, why is there hell? Why good in a world of evil? Why doesn't good stand alone? Why above, why below? The answer, witches, is that neither light nor dark may exist alone. When the world was created, both were formed simultaneously. Alba et tenebris. All is material and all is eternal. From this fundamental Hermetic principle of the Emerald Tablet comes YOU.

As you peer upon the tree of life, witch, first study it right-side up. Memorize it. Know it. Then discover the Sefirot upside down. The directions cross, like a tarot deck or pentagram, and everything can be turned on its head. Thus the Sefirot and six-pointed star become more significant as they exist in perpetual unity, symmetrically representing this universe in opposites.

Now gaze at symbols. A six-pointed star represents two triangles inverted upon one another. The roots of the tree of life, or Sefirot, similarly appear upon "light," as said in Genesis, light birthed simultaneously with its dark shadowy self below in order to manifest this world. Neither tree nor roots exists alone. Read this arcana.

What I'm trying to explain to you, witch, is that darkness, said to be first in Genesis, automatically manifested itself upon its birth with light. "From above, so below." In this world, neither side can exist without the other. Two "pillars." Arcana.

And so too this dichotomous principle spouts forth the seed for the gender principle.

When discussing gender, understand that I am not referring to the literal anatomical presentation of a pussy or penis. This principle involves energies, and its description is from an older time when gender "represented" interpreted elements of male and female. Don't be deceived by literal interpretation or you risk falling into the same curse as I did.

Gender energy is manifested like the sword versus the goblet, hard versus soft, independent versus group, yin versus yang, etc. This principle ebbs and flows, forming our perceived world. Recall that the gender force is such a strong fundamental force in nature that it makes up the entire "sword" and "goblet" categories in the seventy-eight-card tarot deck.

In my study as a magus (male) or witch (female) at Hawthorne, I tried to create "gender" balance in my coven. Initially this was easy. Cadence was achieved in love with my husband, Liam. Liam was the counterbalance for my female magic. He was my opposite partner. Initially, I kept him ignorant of our ways, using him like the scapegoat for Azazel. But as I progressed in deeper studies of Trismegistus, Abramelin, Agrippa, Levi, Newton, and Crowley, I discovered myself to be lacking as a sorceress. I felt the need for a companion in my magic "kal" journey. This was my gravest error. My solution gave me everything I ever desired in magic, while taking away everything I needed in life.

It broke me...

· · ·

Her writing stops. So does her voice. I feel as if she stopped to step outside and cry, or something. It's weird. But I feel really sad too. So sad.

This is difficult…

But her voice returns with that same cold, stoic *Alondraesque* professionalism that I've learned to loathe.

You must understand, my entire drive in life was dedicated to one goal, a goal that was higher than love. I loved my husband more than myself, but, you see, I loved the occult so much more.

Soon I indoctrinated Liam into the ancient rites of magick. Not just my rites, the rites of the ancient magus. I found Liam, just like myself, a very apt and adept pupil. Liam was soon my equal, my green god, my penis and phallus. With me as the witch, the pussy and receptacle, the three-faced goddess, I felt our black and white magic would finally balance Hawthorne. We existed as a manifestation of Baphomet him/herself. A herm-aphrodite if you will: Hermes and Aphrodite. I was finally whole in witchcraft.

At first, it was easy for him to accept our rites in the coven. We were married and it was not so difficult for my husband, Liam, to perform sexual acts publicly in the interest of spiritual energy for our group. But as the ropes of our handfasting weakened, things became troubled.

Need I explain further, Cadence? The price of occult exploration was the greatest sacrifice I have ever made in my life. But it was not the sacrifice of my soul, as so many of the dull-witted fear. No. It was far worse. I gave Hecate everything I had as a person: my friends, my lover. For Hecate, I birthed Luciferianism. First it consumed me. Then it took the thing I loved the most. My husband. Liam.

Of course, before Liam left, he left me a trifle: his best friend, Will Reardon. Soon Bill became a substitute Hermetic magus, teaching Liam's best friend the same magickal arts under Hecate, both white and dark magick. And, just as Liam had done before, we practiced sex magic in the circle until I finally birthed my cure. You, Cadence.

Cadence, after you came to Hawthorne you became not only my disciple, you became my daughter, my balance... I had forgotten happiness until I found you. After the sacrifice of so many students upon my sacred altar, I could not conceive from all these sex acts. I was left barren. Diseased. But, alas, on that same altar, through sex between male and female energies and their sacrifice, I finally could birth a child. You. Thus the magic rituals of our sisters were not for nothing. My daughter was born.

"YOU FUCKING BITCH!"

Goety. Goety. Goety.

I jump up and slam the table with my palms.

"Liam brought his *best friend*, Professor Reardon, to rape my *best friend!?* I'm not your daughter! I'd rather die!"

Goety. Goety. Goety.

Yes, child, cast Alondra upon the cross. Leave sin for Alondra. Good riddance to her.

The words are whispered all around me. It's quiet but seems loud. It's Escoba's voice.

I throw my book closed.

That stops the whispering.

Then I dip my head into my hands and run my fingers

through my long hair. I had felt so happy hearing my teacher's voice. I really miss her! But then she spoke of sex, using disgusting, vile words shrouded under the infamous guise of fucking professionalism.

Sex magick birthed me, Alondra? Really? Rituals of virgin sacrifice between Bill Reardon and innocent young girls? But it wasn't for pleasure, was it? Yeah, you sure did poison me, Alondra. You poisoned everyone. *I'm not your daughter. I fucking hate you!*

A bunch of books are gathered up across the room. The student who was quietly studying is quickly throwing her stuff into her bag and doing everything she can to not meet my gaze. *Oops,* I shouted too loud, I think. What crazy stuff was I saying? I was so mad, I don't even know. She must think I'm a total loon. (I mean, you probably think I am.)

"*Bitch!*" I snap quietly to myself. I was thinking of Alondra, but that does it for the girl. She rushes out of the room.

I clench my fists, take a deep breath, and stare outside again. A white fog is rolling through the branches in the trees. Is my rage changing the weather? Well, the beautiful view a couple floors below calms me a little. But I feel tears forming in my eyes.

How many times do I have to cry over the pain you caused me, teacher? I loved you. Yes, sure, like...like a mother. Maybe. But, as usual, you're making me feel like total shit.

So you poisoned Liam? Of course you did. Then you brought Reardon. Or...Liam brought Reardon? God, is that any better? I liked Liam, but now you tell me Reardon was his *best friend*?

I look through the window, and the fog is glowing under the yellow streetlights. I catch a glimpse of a dark figure in a black robe and a shirtless man rushing down the pathway. Otherwise, the shadowed walkway is empty this late at night. She's a witch in a black cloak with a hood over her head, and she's transparent. A ghost? Wait a minute... No... I think it's Alondra! I'm seeing Alondra's spirit! Maybe I was so pissed that I finally cast her out? Good! Good fucking riddance! Cast Jumbee under the cross and grace of God, you know.

Jumbee. Jumbee. Jumbee.

The dark witch is carrying a large sack over her shoulder. But much weirder, the pale shirtless man, wearing long baggy pants and boots, is walking briskly beside her. She's guiding him by the arm with her free hand. They're rushing down our concrete walkway, around bushes and under tall trees. The man accompanying her is transparent too.

I throw my computer in my leather bag, toss in a few lighter books—*Broomstick* of course—and leave the borrowed books on the table. I'm packing my stuff nearly as fast as that freaked-out student packed hers.

Then I sprint through the large hall, cross a few corridors, and leap down the moving steps of the escalator.

4

CHASING GHOSTS

Racing through the automatic sliding glass doors, I'm strangely met with heat against my cheeks. The weather's so weird this time of year. It was cold on our Sabbath a few nights ago; now it's warm like summer tonight.

Running down the winding concrete walkway, I slow down when it bifurcates into two dirt paths under a deeper forest canopy. Have I lost her?

Shit!

No, there she is! I catch a black robe in the shadows through the branches.

I pull out my cellphone from my pants pocket and call Bryce. But all I hear is a ring tone. I swear, I never know what the hell my husband's up to lately. I make my next call on speed dial.

"Maddie?"

"Hey, Kates," Maddie sounds chirpy as always. "How are you? You know, Kenosha thinks we got just enough recruits for the coven this year, especially after our special guest arrived. I knew Adder's outburst would help get them excited. And did you hear about Mira?"

"Maddie?"

"Hmm? What? You sound upset. You okay?"

"I'm following a ghost."

"Huh?"

"I'm following a ghost. I'm chasing Alondra."

There's silence on the other end. For a moment, I think she hung up on me. All I hear is the sound of leaves crunching under my boots. I'm cutting through bushes and dodging trees around the trail to catch up to her.

"You're chasing Alondra?" Maddie finally asks. "How?"

"Or some other ghost? I'm not sure. If it's Alondra, I tell you, I'm going to give her a piece of my mind. You know what, Maddie? I think I should disband our coven. I don't know why I never thought about this before. Why would I take over a coven that did such horrible things? Horrible things to you? I think Alondra poisoned us. Maybe Reardon wasn't always bad, maybe he was poisoned by her too?"

"Cadence, what the hell are you talking about? You need to calm down."

"Liam did those same sick things Reardon did. Can you believe that! And now we're recruiting new students! Why? I mean, why the fuck are we doing that? So Bryce, our high wizard, my husband, can have ceremonial sex with fresh, innocent young recruits? Is that the plan, Madison? I mean, Bryce *claims* he only had sex with Enora, but who knows what Mr. Billington does when he's alone at home in the Billington House? You know what I mean? He's probably out fucking like a total goety. Good riddance to him, I tell you, Maddie. Goety. Goety. Goety."

"Cadence," she drawls carefully, "you're sounding really weird. Bryce and I love being witches. We love it for the craft, not for *sex*. How many times do I have to go over this with you. The past is the past. You brought us out of it and cleaned everything up. You're not talking like yourself."

"I know. But really, if any of us should be mad, I'd think it should be you. I mean, all the bad stuff happened to you, not me."

"Well, now you're making me mad, Cadence."

And she stops talking. I leap over a large fallen tree branch and twist my ankle. *Ow! Shit, that hurt! Ow!*

"Babe, where are you?" she asks. "You need help. You're talking like you're under a curse again."

"I'm not under a curse," I say, panting. "Did you know that Liam did the same shit as Professor Reardon?"

"What shit?"

"Sex magick," I say in disgust. "Ugh. Sacrificial *sex magick*, Maddie! I'm so disgusted. I'm so—" My voice breaks. "Upset."

Goety. Goety. Goety.

Just when I'm about to catch up to Alondra, she and the man she's leading veer off the cement path. Then she passes through tree trunks. I know this area well enough to know that Alondra is heading up the hills overlooking campus toward Hilltop Bluff. I think I can catch up to her.

"You still there, Cadence? Tell me where you are. Tell me. Who the hell cares what Liam did?"

"Not sure there's time, Maddie." I catch my breath. And now my ankle's killing me. I mean, I'm totally out of shape, but my ankle's now killing me. I used to work out every night, but not much lately. Guess it's not so easy chasing ghosts. "Well, at least you're putting me at ease. This obviously isn't a witch wandering if I can call you on the phone. It's just those words, you know."

"What words?"

"*Sex magick.* It drives me nuts. I read Alondra talking about it in my book again and it made me crazy. And then the bitch told me how much she loved me, you know like a daughter. Because now, you know, I was born as her witch-child under her sex magick rituals from sacrificing all those innocent students that sick fuck Reardon touched. Or God, Maddie, *Liam* touched. So now, you know, I can carry on sex rituals as her demon child. I mean, she told me Liam brought Reardon. Did you know that? Can you believe that?"

"Were you...having sex with Liam in a vision again?"

"*What!* No. Gross. Did you know, Maddie, did you know Bill Reardon was *Liam's friend?*"

"Cadence, you're chasing Alondra? How? Just stop following her."

"I told you, I'm chasing her. But...did you know Reardon was Liam's best friend?"

"Stop it, Cadence. I don't care. Who are you chasing? How can you be chasing Alondra?"

"Doesn't it make you think a little less of him? Alondra said Liam was involved in those same sick sex practices, Maddie."

"Liam killed a little girl. He brought a whole house down on Winona. He's not a good man. And Alondra's past is not our coven anymore. You're running our coven. The coven is yours and you've stopped all that. We've talked about this over and over."

"Is that any better? I mean, *Reardon*, Maddie? *Fucking Bill Reardon was Liam's best friend!*"

I squint at a sudden burst of light and crash of thunder. The bolt seemed only a few feet from me, nearly knocking me down.

"*Is that from your casting, Cadence! Where are you?*"

"Where's my husband! You tell me that first, Maddie! Who the hell is he with? 'Fess up! I know he's up to no good. Tell me who he's with tonight."

"Huh?"

"Where's Bryce! I called and he didn't answer his phone. Is Jo out fucking? Is that what he's doing? If you know where Josiah is, Maddie, and you're hiding it, I swear, Madison, I will never forgive you."

There's another strike of lightning. This one nearly hits me.

My ears ring. It takes a second for my eyes to readjust.

I rub them. It's a bit blurry, but I see Alondra passing over the surface of a brook. So I leap from one stone to the other, crossing the brook. But then I land on my bad ankle. *Shit!* That makes my other foot splash in the water. I nearly lose my cellphone. I don't, but my bag is hurled into some bushes across the water.

Ow! My ankle's killing me!

A white fog is thickening around the dirt trail, covered by the forest canopy, as I climb the hillside. It's getting darker, shrouded by all the wisps of white mist.

"Cadence!" Maddie cries. "Cadence!"

"Hmm? What? I think Abigail's coven needs to be disbanded. Cast Jumbee under the cross and the grace of God, you know, Maddie? That's all I'm saying. Please, Jesus, take this gris-gris away. Cast it out and leave sin for Alondra. I don't know why I didn't see it before. Alondra is like a total goety, Madds. A total goety, I tell you. A goety. Goety, goety, goety."

"Cadence, tell me where you're at now!"

"Willow's just as bad, I think. How do you know who's good anymore? What's going to...what's going to stop me from..."

But there's no time to talk. I'm searching through leaves and branches, looking for my leather book bag. When I find it under all the twigs and leaves, I sling it over my shoulder and, ignoring all the pain in my leg, I rush back onto the narrow path.

I'm slower, now limping a little. My ankle hurts so bad, but I have to catch up. Soon, I find that the narrow trail is high enough that a few wrong steps could send me plummeting a hundred feet to my death.

"Bye, Maddie. Gotta go."

"Wait! Wait! No! I'll meet you, Kate. Just tell me where you are."

"Hilltop Bluff. I'm not scared. This isn't a curse. These are my hallowed grounds. But I do feel like Liam sure has a lot of explaining to do. He's just as bad as she was, I think. I mean, Reardon? *Reardon!?* Reardon was Liam's best friend! Can you believe it! I really liked Liam. If this is Alondra's ghost, I'm sure going to talk to her. You know, cast Jumbee out and leave the sin for Alondra. I'm gonna get her. I've had it with Alondra, Maddie!"

"Cadence, how can you be chasing Alondra! Alondra's been inside you."

"*I think Josiah is cheating on me, Maddie!*" I scream. "*God, where is he! If you know, you better tell me! Tell me where Bryce is NOW!*"

"Cadence! Calm down. Just, just, stay on the phone and I'll come right over and—"

I hang up on her.

Mwen met, gris-gris nan Alondra.

I'm climbing up the trail, almost at the top of the hill. It's brighter up there, as if the fog is clearing at the top of the hillside.

Mambo Escoba helps what is mine, child.

5

___

THE MAYPOLE

AT THE CREST OF THE HILL, I CATCH ALONDRA IN THE CENTER OF a field, tying that man to a wooden stake. I was expecting to see more witches, but it's just Alondra and the bare-chested man in the center of a large grassy glade. He is pale-skinned and has a beard. She crouches under him and runs dark-gloved fingers over the logs. It magically lights a shallow violet flame. Sparks of light crackle around the man's pants and boots, and he looks down, but the purple flames don't seem to burn. He doesn't care about the fire. He just stares at her. He seems spellbound by her.

"Alondra?" I ask, moving closer.

The witch ignores me, slowly removing her dark gloves, one finger at a time. Under the flickering light, her hands look as black as the glove. Wait...this can't be Alondra. Alondra has very pale skin.

The witch comes right up to the man's face, standing in the fire, and puts her arms around him, kissing his lips passionately. He's a strong man, with well-built arms, nearly twice her size. They laugh as they make out over the violet bonfire. Then she lets her cloak drop, revealing a naked dark-skinned body.

The flames don't bother them at all. It acts like a purple filter for my eyes, causing their transparent bodies to contort and twist, as if they're a part of the fire.

She lifts an index finger, pushing away from his chest. Then she takes a clear bottle from her bag. She pours the contents in a circle around the stake and bonfire. I remember Enora doing this to me before her blindfold spell in the park, but this woman is doing it while swaying, as if dancing to music. Then she comes right up to him and spits in his face.

My phone rings. I reach down into my pocket and shut it off.

The witch is back to making out with him. Her fingers untie a thin rope holding up his trousers and they slip off. Then she kneels down and pulls off his boots. Now they're both naked—her dark body and his pale one—close together in a purple-filtered light.

She drinks from her bottle and spits the contents at his face again. The spitting doesn't upset him. It makes him open his eyes wide, as if it is making him hungrier.

I turn away. I know what they're up to next and this is indecent. It's reminding me of that time I watched Liam and Alondra in my living room.

Gazing back down the hill, I can't find my path. Though it's clear in the glade, a white fog has formed in the night, blocking the view of campus below. I think it's white, but in darkness with the flickering purple flames, it's glowing violet.

"Jo, you are mine by magic," the witch breathes. "Yes? You, me, we. Gris-gris does this? Jumbee? Or is it love?"

"Love," he says, closing his eyes, nodding. "It's love, Essie."

"You love this witch?" she asks in a whisper with a chuckle. "Love me? I've been through this before, I have. Why should I trust you? I was loved by master in Bulbancha. Some say he died of black vomit. Then I was accused of cursing. Now you're saying you love me? Billington master loves Escoba? How can I trust you?"

"Because I love you."

"It's a big risk to me, Jo," she says quietly, shaking her head. "All right. If you love me, as you say, then bless me. Bless Escoba by the fire. Free her and name her Hawthorn after the tree. If your love be true, name her Hawthorn after the May flower. Here, you be my maypole, my man, and I your vessel. Call me Hawthorn. You love Escoba Hawthorn like your misses? Love this witch by rite. Bless me, love me, and I love you too, Jo. I do, I mean it. I swear it upon my loa. Upon blessed Erzulie, I swear. For I love you so much, forever and ever, too, I do, Jo."

"All right."

"You're crazy, Josiah," she says, bursting out laughing and shaking her head. "You know that? You're crazy!"

He laughs too. But then he quickly loses his smile, shaking his head. She presses her lips almost violently to his, embracing him so close. Then she runs her hand through his short hair and down his back. Their bodies flicker naked in lilac and indigo.

But she shoves him away once more, dancing, running her hands along the curves of her naked hips, breasts, and ass.

"If we do it, we do this my way," she says, dancing and cocking her head back, "but I give you one last chance. By Erzulie." She turns her back to him, raising her arms and closing her eyes. "You still want her?"

"No, Essie, I want *you*."

She dips down, shaking her head, and laughs again, in dance. Then she grabs her bottle and guzzles more than ever.

She spits it at his feet.

"Hawthorn," she says. "Hawthorn. Dance around. You, me, Jo, upon maypole. Love me. Bless me. Wrap me round. Dance with me. Escoba Hawthorn leaves fall under Damballa. Then

Damballa, blessed serpent, comes to Erzulie. Come. Come. Blessed be Cadence. Cadence Hawthorn. Hawthorn. Blessed be as Cadence Hawthorne."

And then Escoba runs her fingers over his hard chest and over his legs. And she touches his cock.

I quickly try to turn again. But I can't.

She puts her breasts right under his face. Then she rises, extending her arms in dance, spitting more liquid at him. She laughs. The spit still doesn't repel him. It seems to arouse him even more, making him stare more hungrily.

She reaches down into her bag and brings out a long yellow snake. She pets the snake's head, kisses it, and dances gracefully with the snake around her neck. She brings the serpent up to his lips. He kisses it and closes his eyes, moaning in ecstasy.

"You won't tell?" she asks with a chuckle, still under him. "You won't tell, will you? You promise you won't tell? Misses is my friend, Jo. I love her too."

"Promise."

"I warn you." She nods, standing up. Then, with palms up, she dances before him again.

"Escoba?" I ask. "Escoba?"

"*Goety*," she answers, shaking her head, still dancing before Josiah. "*Goety*. *Goety*. Damballa comes to Erzulie. You are mine. Not Alondra's. Why do you listen to her? Not Cadence Billington. Cadence Hawthorne. Understand."

Then she collapses on the dirt, shaking, as if convulsing, under the man. I smell a scent of roses. It's pleasant. Josiah isn't disturbed. It's like being spat at—he seems enraptured. It's almost as if he expected it. After a few more shakes, Escoba stands straight. She cocks her head back at me then sticks up her nose.

She struts back to Josiah with her head held high. She runs her hands along his naked chest and runs her tongue along his beard.

"You want woman with perfume and scented oils, Jo?" she asks quietly by his ear. "Nice smells? Skin as white as the moon? You want Erzulie, not Escoba, Josiah. Eh? Erzulie."

"No, I want you, Essie," he says, shaking his head. "I told you, I want you, Escoba."

"Escoba?" she asks, shaking her head. "No Escoba. Erzulie."

"Escoba Hawthorn. For Hawthorne. Yes, I will set you free. I will. I swear it, Essie. Because I love you."

"So you say," she says with a nod. "But I've been tricked before."

She turns her back toward him, dancing slowly now, running her naked back over his front while touching the curves of her breasts. Then she lowers herself against him, extending her arms to the sky. I look up and see a full white moon and then back down at the fog in the field. The white smoke blows gently over the cliff, mixing with purple.

"Erzulie," she whispers, swaying gracefully back and forth before his naked body. "Erzulie. Bless this, slave owner. Slave? Love? Blessed be, free me, Damballa. Erzulie show love for Josiah Billington. It all be for Cadence, you know."

"Untie me, Essie," he breathes, shaking his head. "Please, Essie. I want to feel your skin. Please. I so want to touch you."

"No," she says with a laugh. "No, I won't."

She picks up the yellow snake again, kissing it. Then she brings it up to him. He kisses the snake so violently that he seems ready to bite its head off.

"Please," he exclaims. "I don't want Erzulie! I want you, Essie. Change back."

She laughs more than ever. Then she shakes her head and runs her index finger over his lips.

"See?" she asks, shaking her head, and she kisses his lips again. "See, our love is true. Blessed love by Erzulie in the cross-roads. Come, flower, if your lust is true, you are now mine. Take Escoba Hawthorne. Give seed by the May flower. It be wrong, but is it wrong if it's for love? The same as a bee to a flower. Damballa to Erzulie. Is love ever wrong if you love one another? Does it bring the stench of decay, or the fragrance of flowers?"

There's a flash like lightning. But I don't hear thunder. Then I smell a horrible stench of rotting meat.

Escoba steps back a few paces after another burst of light. She makes hand signals as if casting a spell. These seem like occult symbols, but the lightning and flickering purple flames flash too fast for me to read them. I'm trying hard to decipher the shapes, thinking that if I can, I can understand what the hell this vision means.

Then she grabs him hard and kisses him again.

"Escoba!" I shout. "Escoba? Why are you showing me this?"

She backs her ass up against him, her breasts bobbing before her crouched body. Then he pushes his hips forward. He's still tied to the pole, but he's pushing into her body. From her moaning, I can tell he's fucking her now. The violet flames grow and dominate the fog again. The flames aren't burning the couple, but the flickering purple light sends out sparks and flashes brightly over their bodies.

I try to turn away again. This is indecent. But it takes all my strength just to nudge my head an inch.

Their bodies move at unnatural speed, as if someone pressed fast forward on a tape. Then they stop, with her naked body still pressed against him.

"Untie me," I hear him say, breathlessly, in the wind. "Please untie me. Please, Essie. I want to touch you. I want to feel you. You feel so good. But I want to touch your skin with my hands. I want to feel your chest and skin. I love you so."

She nods and faces him. Then she dips down and takes that bottle, pouring more of the clear contents of the bottle over her tits, hips, and ass. She dances again with her nude body touching and sliding along him, skin to skin, her skin wet from whatever she poured over herself. But then she walks around the wooden pole and unties his hands. When freed, he quickly grabs her hard. She laughs. He's twice her size and he easily lifts her whole body, holding her by her ass, and then pushes into her again. And then they're back to making love.

I can't turn away. I can't. It's not right to watch, but it's like they're making me look. And she's laughing at me, as if taunting me.

I hear their bodies slap as I watch his hands squeeze her butt hard. He moves her up and down with those thick, powerful arms. He is twice her size, and she's easily carried against his muscular chest.

I feel so aroused.

The violet light becomes so bright that I have to squint. Cries of ecstasy surround me, echoing from every tree branch and leaf. I can't see. Now I can only hear their sex.

I blink and blink, trying to open my eyes.

They've stopped. Escoba is in his tight embrace, panting.

"Don't ever break this spellbinding," she whispers. "Don't you ever cross me, Jo. Or love will turn to ruin."

"I will always love you," he says, still breathless.

"Next time we go fucking in the woods, it be in two moons," she continues in a whisper. "You release me after and get me my freedom? You promise. Free me as Cadence."

"I promise, Essie."

"Call me Hawthorn for the tree. Free me as Cadence Hawthorne, birthed upon the May flower by Damballa and Erzulie tonight."

"Hawthorne," he says with a nod.

"Hawthorne," she says.

Escoba turns her head to me, still in his embrace. Then I feel that grima I felt with Cordelia at my house.

"Follower of Hecate," she says, looking into my eyes, "not of dirt, nor bird, nor fire. You are snake, my darling. Damballa.

Abigail goes by crossroads. Good riddance to her. As she leaves, you are free. Hawthorn leaves for Hawthorne. Ask Escoba, child, what loa harms you? When eyes open in darkness, they cannot see. Yes? But in light, they see. Darkness shades. It shadows your world. Those in darkness cannot see, but with light, you will see shadows. When you finally see what I see, go show the rest of them."

And she lets go of Josiah, guzzles down the rest of the clear liquid from the bottle, and charges at me spitting all the contents at my face.

6

FRIENDS

I'M ON MY KNEES NEAR THE EDGE OF A LONG ROCK AT THE farthest point on Hilltop Bluff looking down over the university. The fog has lifted. Down below, beyond all those trees, I can just make out the lights from our library, where I was studying. I could walk down the forest path and make my way back home, but I think I'm just trying to make sense of all the craziness I just witnessed.

What the hell was that? Why did I see it? I was angry with Alondra, not Escoba. But is Escoba's spirit, my ancestor, fighting Alondra's ghost inside me, like the witch council told me?

It's hard to catch my breath. I think I'm in shock.

Now that the fog has dispersed, the moon is bright and the light feels as if it warms me. It's a nice evening, ironically. And, as a witch, the beauty of the outdoors soothes me. It grounds me.

What was I doing? Studying Eliphas Levi in the library? No, I was listening to my infernal teacher, Alondra. Well, if she considers me her daughter, I suppose I *am* under an ancestor curse. Because I have no interest in ever making peace with that beast. Maybe the triumvirate of the witch council was right all along.

I hear the chirping of crickets amid my heart pounding in my ears. That's nice.

"Cadence! Cadence!"

Shit, I nearly fell over the edge of the cliff! Maddie's yelling made me nearly fall off!

"What, Maddie! You almost killed me!"

"Cadence." She is rushing over, out of breath. My brother, Damie, is right behind her. "Oh, Cadence, thank God you're okay. We came as quickly as we could."

"I'm fine," I say, getting up. "Almost died from your yelling, though."

Maddie throws her arms around me—away from the ledge, of course.

"Oh, I was so worried, babe," she whispers in my ear. "Are you sure you're okay?"

"Yes, I'm fine. But I told you. You almost made me fall off the cliff."

"Serves you right, Cadence!" she exclaims, backing up and slapping my shoulder. "You freaked me out! You said you were chasing Alondra, but I knew it wasn't her. Who was it?"

"How'd you know it wasn't her?"

"Just tell me," she insists, shaking her head.

"Escoba."

"Oh, thank god," Maddie says, clutching her chest in relief.

"Why is Escoba better?" I ask with a laugh.

"She was worried it was Enora, Kates," Damie says.

"Remember Cordelia, dope?" asks Maddie patronizingly. "Remember her coven is threatening us? I thought Enora was casting another curse on you and was having you follow her to hurt you."

"This is my hallowed ground," I say, shaking my head. "Aamon's curse died when he died."

She touches my face and sniffs her fingers.

"Eww. What is this? What's that gross smell on you? It smells like...alcohol." She shows me a wet finger. "Have you been drinking, Cadence? You can't be drinking. You're expecting."

"No."

"Then why is your face wet?" Maddie smells her fingers again. "It...it smells like whiskey or something."

Then I feel so creeped out. I'm almost too scared to answer her.

"What's the matter?" Maddie asks, opening her eyes wide.

"Rum," I say with a slow nod, folding my arms and turning back to the rocky ledge. "I think. I mean, I think it's rum."

I touch my wet face and flick drops from my hands. My forehead and long hair are wet too. I hadn't realized it before. I reach into my leather bag for a small bag of tissues and wipe down my forehead and cheeks. The liquid is all over me. I hope it was just rum and not some weird black witch-concoction. But rum is hardly comforting either. Escoba lived two hundred years ago, you know.

"Why do you have rum on your face if you didn't drink?" asks Maddie.

"Maybe I am in a curse, Maddie? Yeah, how can I have this stuff on my face? I don't recall touching alcohol."

"What was Escoba, that ghost, doing here?" Maddie asks.

"Having sex. I watched her take Josiah Billington up to the top of this hill, rope him to a pole, and then make love to him. She called the stake a maypole."

"Why not?" Damien asks with a shrug.

My stupid brother has this huge grimace. Maddie slugs his shoulder. I don't think it's very funny either.

"I felt compelled to watch," I say.

"I would too," Damie quips.

"Shut up, Damie!" Maddie snaps. "It's not funny. She's... I

mean—" Maddie's voice breaks. "We're really freaked out right now, okay."

"Sorry, Madds."

But then my brother embraces her and kisses her cheek. Gross.

"Why were you watching them have sex, Cadence?" Maddie asks.

"I think she wanted me to watch. I was furious when I saw Alondra telling me I was her daughter in *Broomstick*. I think my anger tipped me into a wandering. Maybe Escoba was staking her territory, or something? Telling me I'm not Alondra's daughter, I'm *hers*? It felt like she was marking her territory. *I am* hers, in a way. You and I, Damie, are part of her family."

They're just looking at me really weird. Do you blame them?

"But I also witnessed Escoba's freedom. Maybe she had sex with Josiah, her master, to get freed? I don't know. It's all so fucking weird. But... Josiah kept repeating that he loved her. And, Damie, she was also showing me how we got our last name. It's from the tree, Damien. The maypole tree. The hawthorn tree. Our last name is taken from the may flower on Beltane. The 'e' must have been added later or something."

"Cadence, this is great," Maddie says, "but what the hell does any of this have to do with alcohol all over your face?"

"Escoba spit on me."

"A ghost spit on you?" asks my brother with eyes wide. "How can a ghost spit on you?"

"I don't know, Damie! How the fuck should I know?"

Maddie rubs my back. I shrug her off and stand closer to the ledge (farther away from the edge this time to not fall off).

"We need to go call Mira or something and ask her," I say. "She loves this kind of weird shit."

"Cadence!" cries Bryce. "Cadence, are you all right!"

He rushes over. He throws his arms around me, hugging me so tight.

"Oh, Bryce," I say. "God, Bryce, I was scared." I run my hand through his hair. "Bryce, I love you, okay?"

"You were scared?" Bryce snaps. "How do you think we felt? Maddie told me it could be Enora! Was it?"

"It was just a vision," I reply. "Bryce, I really love you, okay?"

"Sure, Katie, sure," Bryce says. "But what happened?"

"Never mind. Can we just go home?"

"What's that smell, Cadence?" Bryce asks. "Are you drinking? You can't drink. You're—"

"I know, I know," I say with a sigh. "I wasn't drinking. A ghost just spit on me."

7

OUROBOROS

IT'S COLD OUTSIDE. EVEN WEARING MY PITCH-BLACK ROBE OVER two shirts and a sweater by our lovely bonfire isn't warm enough. Yep, from the hot night with my bizarre ancestor vision to this cold evening, it's typical unpredictable Georgia weather. Very soon we pass from Litha to Mabon.

And right now, there's a band of spooked kids with eyes wide open sitting around the bonfire on white plastic chairs. They are introducing themselves. Many have no idea what they're in for with all our ceremony stuff.

Mira's already taken a liking to one of our new witches, Abella, an intimidating-looking girl. She is broad-shouldered, bald, and pale with a large black sigil of Lucifer tattooed on her neck. Yeah, Abella's Satanic. Mira's not into Satanism, but she loves the girl's magical enthusiasm, I think. Anyway, there's no doubt Abella told our two new Asian recruits, shy Nancy and her boisterous bestie, Beth, and all the rest of them about what we're about. I figure the girls got the 411 they needed from her or Mira. But, across the bonfire, Kenosha's ignoring this fact, acting as if the new recruits don't know anything.

"I want all of you to log onto the campus portal and get

familiar with your messaging basket," Kenosha says. She's wigless and wearing a forest-green cloak. "You can message Cadence directly. But in this circle around this bonfire, you can just call Mr. and Mrs. Wallace Bryce and Cadence. They lead this special school program."

I mean, I totally agree with Mira. It's time to stop the charade.

Mira grunts. She's real pissed. I suppose it's good to finally see a witch more upset with Kenosha than I am.

"Cadence, you're the High Priestess," Mira snaps. "We have to talk about what happened on Hilltop Bluff the other night. We have to discuss this now. Our coven is in danger." Then she turns to Kenosha. "We have to speak of *witchcraft*, not the latest school protocols or assignments. We need to talk about our coven."

"Raven, this isn't only an initiation," objects Kenosha, "it's an introduction to the special metaphysical history honors program. Many of our new recruits are first years and—"

"So, this is a real witch group?" asks Beth innocently. "It's not just an honors program to study ritual?"

"Uh, yeah," Abella says, rolling her eyes. "I told you they're real witches, Beth. Actually, I was already a real witch. That's why I joined."

"You guys need to know that Windstorm, or Cadence here, had a vision," Mira says. "She saw Escoba and Josiah together up on Hilltop Bluff. She saw her ancestor. It was after Alondra spoke with her about what we were doing before—"

"Raven," Kenosha interrupts. "Many of the students don't even believe in visions."

"Kenosha!" Mira exclaims. "Shit, just stop it! This is stupid. Adder showed up during your orientation meeting at this house. She claimed Cadence was attacking their dreams with spells and magic. Didn't all of these new recruits hear her?"

"We have to indoctrinate them slowly," Kenosha says, shaking her head.

"Windstorm," Mira seethes between her teeth, turning to me. "What does our High Priestess, our *leader*, think?"

"Tell everyone everything," I say with a shrug, folding my arms. Kenosha scowls. I straighten my robe. "Everything, Mira. We keep no secrets in our circle anymore."

"Some things must remain secret, Windstorm," Kenosha objects. "You know this, Raven, better than any of us. You are now a member of the council. And some of our recruits might not stay here long if they know everything."

"Secrecy is for *outside* the circle, Willow," Mira replies. "Not within this coven."

"We have to go slow," Kenosha says.

"There's no time!" Mira objects.

"So we're going to be like real witches?" asks Noori, a dark-skinned Indian girl.

"Yeah, dope," says Maddie. "Real." But then she laughs. "What the hell's wrong with saying we're real practicing witches, Kenosha?"

"Nothing," Kenosha says. "But I don't think we should discuss the history of your teacher with the newcomers. Going over Cadence's current problems is going to bring it up. I think we should speak about your vision in private this time, Cadence. We must be patient, or some of our sisters are going to leave. And then, Mira, they're going to tell others *outside*."

Mira looks at me, raising an eyebrow. "Everything, High Priestess?"

I nod to her.

"How much do you guys know?" Mira asks. Then she asks Bryce, sitting beside me. "How much did you tell them during your *honors* dinner?"

"We already know we're here to practice real magic," says Abella. "Everybody's hush hush on campus, but many, like myself, actually came to this school to be let into this occult program. Like I said, I was already a witch before I joined—" She puts two fingers up. "This 'honors' program."

"What type of witch were you?" Mira asks with a chuckle. "Wiccan?"

"Luciferian," she says, shaking her head. "I'm a chaos magician. I've been practicing since grade school. I can tell you all anything you want to know about Luciferianism and Thelemic principles. I've read extensive passages from the Hermetic Order of the Golden Dawn and from the *Book of the Law*."

"If you're a Satanist," Mira says with a nod, "your beliefs won't sit well with Cadence. She has this total hang up about good versus evil."

"You do too, Meer," says Courtney, beside her.

"Not really," Mira says with a laugh. Then she looks across the fire at Bryce. "Have you shown them any real spellcasting yet, High Wizard?"

"Willow recommended we start slow," Bryce says.

"Cordelia knew her risks coming here," Mira says. "That's how desperate their Abaddon coven is becoming. There's no time to be careful. We have to talk about the dangers *now* and think of magic for protection. The question is, who's attacking them? You, Katie?" I vehemently shake my head. "Willow, you wanted Katie's Ekimmu exorcised. We might need to consider this again. We have to do something."

Kenosha takes a deep breath. "The new students might not even believe in ghost possession."

"I do," quips Abella with a smile.

But Beth and Nancy just look at each other uncomfortably. Mira turns to Gail, a girl with long blond hair. Gail just looks down.

"'Fraid introductions are over, girls," Mira says. "This circle is a real witch coven, a *real* coven, the most powerful in America." Abella smiles wide. The other newbies just nod, looking serious. "We meet here on our Sabbath, every Friday, and cast real magick. Magick with a 'k.' Our leader before Katie was the most knowledgeable sorceress in the world. Alondra. Now this coven, the Hawthorne coven, belongs to Cadence. She isn't knowledgeable like Alondra." Mira smirks. "But she's the most powerful witch I've ever known. Unfortunately, as you all heard from Adder, there's a devil worshipping cult in Atlanta with a leader wanted for murder. Enora. They wish to curse each and every member of this circle now."

Mira looks at Beth and Nancy. They nod, not looking surprised. Noori and Gail still look down. Kenosha just looks pissed. Mira pauses, pensive for a moment. Then she turns to me.

"What did you see on Hilltop Bluff, Cadence? Maddie told me she found you there with your face drenched in alcohol. She says Escoba spit on you. That's some pretty intense divination. What did you see? Please tell the group, High Priestess."

"Escoba was with her enslaver, Josiah, on our hills above campus," I reply with a nod. "I was seeing the past, two hundred years ago." Okay, that makes Beth and Nancy cringe. "Escoba told me that the town was hers. And that *I'm* hers. She showed me that the town, and my family, was named after the hawthorn tree. The maypole tree. I almost felt like I wasn't scrying anything with my magic. Rather, Escoba's spirit was showing me that she was my great-great-grandmother. She was taking ownership of my family, even though Alondra's related to me distantly too."

"When she spoke to you, do you recall any exact words?"

I touch my chin in thought. Then I nod.

"She keeps repeating the same thing. She's been doing it since last Halloween." I pause, trying to remember. "Not of dirt...nor bird, nor fire... Bird isn't your...mambo. Then, this time, she said something vital about shadows and...that I needed to go tell people about them."

"A mambo is a voodoo witch," Kenosha says.

"Yes...but she said '*yours is snake*,'" I interject. "Can you make sense of *snake*, Willow?"

"The snake is your totem, Cadence," answers Kenosha. Then she hesitates, looking at all the new faces in the group. "Do you remember...what Reardon did to you? He didn't choose that totem. You did. Just as Enora's and Mira's totem is a raven, yours is a snake. Falconsong never made your totems, she used her powers to discern what you already were inside."

"She said 'not dirt'?" asks Mira. "So, she's telling you, Cadence, that you're not just an earther, you're a witch. A witch with a snake as a totem. That's a powerful one. But you don't want to be a snake, do you?"

"No, not really."

"You should," Kenosha says.

"Yes." Mira nods.

"Why would Katie want to be a snake?" Maddie asks with a chuckle.

"A snake in voodoo is our most powerful symbol," Kenosha says. "In the Christian religion, it represents Satan, because the snake often represents feral, base phallic desire. That's only one part. But also, just as important, the snake sheds its skin. For witches, this represents renewal and resurrection."

"Ouroboros," Mira says.

"Ouroboros," Kenosha says with a nod. "The Infiniti symbol. Constant regeneration and renewal. The circle. Just like the protective circle we form with chalk before every Sabbath; much like a pentacle or Yin and Yang symbol. Just like the very circle we form when holding ceremony, like tonight, around our fire. It represents enclosure in ritual. Not only do you have an ancestor curse, Cadence, as an earther, you battle the magic within you. You're the most powerful witch I've ever known, a snake, while having the countenance of an earther. A nonbeliever. But, maybe, it's this combination that gives you so much power? It grounds you more than any of us. More than lovers of Hecate, like Mira, Enora, and Alondra—and maybe even me. We love the arts more than anything else, yet you practice with the greatest force."

Mira nods.

Kenosha turns to Noori and Gail and says, "Your first assignment is a report on the ouroboros."

That finally loosens everyone up and we laugh. This is the Kenosha I've learned to like since she's been sick. Even Mira permits a smile.

"But how the hell are you two getting all this from one sentence?" I ask.

"Now you're proving it," Mira says with a chuckle. "There's that infernal disbelief, Kenosha."

"Yes, Mira," Kenosha says. "Agreed. New initiates, your High Priestess is powerful, but a very stubborn witch."

"Sure," I say, "but what does—"

"Just a second, so the last part, Cadence..." Mira puts a hand up and looks up to the clear, starry sky. "Shadows." Mira shakes her head, looking confused. She turns to Kenosha. "That sounds like...necromancy?"

"Perhaps." Kenosha nods slowly.

"The triumvirate said you have two struggles," Mira continues. "One is Samhain, or Melanie, the other is your ancestor curse between Abigail and Escoba. If Samhain's power has diminished, your ancestor curse might be growing. Kenosha told you that you have to get rid of Alondra from inside you. Did anything happen to bring on this vision?"

"Alondra was teaching me about Eliphas Levi in *Broomstick*. She spoke, in *Broomstick*, of how wonderful it was that I was coming to Hawthorne to take over her circle. But then I flipped out when she said she was passing on her tradition..." I look at the newbies again. Maybe Kenosha's right? Maybe they're not ready for me talking about this part of our past? "Our past tradition of *sacrifice*."

"You need to let that shit go, Cadence," Mira says. "You can't help us if you keep going nuts every time sex magic is mentioned."

"Mira, not now!" Kenosha snaps.

"He messed with me and Maddie, and the others," Mira continues, "but you ended it, Cadence. You have to get over it."

But even this doesn't disturb the initiates. Have they heard rumors about all that awful stuff from our past too?

"Cadence was rambling about disbanding the coven over it last night, Mira," Maddie says.

"I was furious," I say with a nod. "But I think I was partly under a spell. I don't want to disband the coven."

"Well, right now calling it quits would be the absolute dumbest thing you could do for Bryce and all your friends here," Mira says. "For me. For Courtney. Kenosha. You need to keep it together now more than ever. You asked me what Escoba was telling you? She's telling you that you're a witch, a powerful one. But, yeah, she's also staking out her territory. She's fighting Alondra. Alondra and Escoba are fighting inside you. It's a struggle that has to end, Cadence. Just like the past."

"I want her out, Mira. But what does she have to do with Enora?"

"I don't know," Mira says. "My worry is that your struggle could be making you cast against Enora without knowing it. We have to get Alondra out of you once and for all. But a spell might not be enough. That nearly killed Kenosha. We have to try something different."

"I was hurt by Melanie," Kenosha says, shaking her head. "We really haven't had a chance to even try my shield spell yet. I disagree. I think we could attempt it again now that our circle is safe."

"Well, I've been thinking something different, Willow. A séance."

"Possibly," says Kenosha with a pensive nod.

"But a séance is dark magic, Cadence," Mira says. "You keep telling everyone how you only want white magic practiced in this circle."

"Will it get rid of Alondra?"

"Maybe," says Kenosha thoughtfully. "The magic I was schooled in, Mira, does not always associate necromancy with evil. The spirit world for us is a part of our world. Séances are acceptable in voodoo. Just as our Summerland ceremonies are accepted. But they can be as silly and useless as Ouija boards."

"A direct communication with Alondra on our terms, not yours, Katie, is an option," Mira says. "And maybe some of the other members of the council could return to help. Maybe Aunt Jane. Or, maybe, even Liam?"

"No, not him!" I snap, shaking my head. "Not Liam!"

Everyone looks at me funny. Honestly, I think I hate him now.

"Okay," Mira drawls. "No Liam then." Then she chuckles. "Cadence, what was Escoba doing with Josiah on Hilltop Bluff, anyway?"

"Conceiving me."

Mira furrows her brow and stares. Kenosha stares too.

"They were, you know—" I look down, gesticulating in the air. Everyone's staring at me like I'm nuts. "They were having... you know, sex."

Mira loses all seriousness and bursts into laughter. She shakes her head and seems to do the best she can to not laugh. No one else is laughing.

"Stop it, Meer," Courtney says very seriously, laying a hand on her leg. "This is serious. It's really affecting Cadence badly."

"Sorry," Mira says. "But this is why Courtney and I want in on this coven again, Cadence." When she finally gets a hold of herself, Mira says, "I'd like you to reinitiate me and Courtney into the Hawthorne coven too. We can be of more help as two of your official witches. We need to join in ceremony with all the new recruits during the initiation ceremony next week."

"Fine. Might need even more recruits if some of the new girls bail after hearing all this crazy stuff."

"No, they don't have a choice," Mira says, turning grave again. "Everyone that chose to gather here is in danger now. They're safer with our magic. That was the other reason I came. I had to warn you, Cadence, of Enora's clairvoyance. See, Courtney and I know she's watching us. And she's been watching you." She turns to Kenosha. "She's scrying again, Willow. In fact—" Mira looks around the surrounding trees—"I think she's watching us now."

Kenosha searches my yard too.

"She's watching us, Mira?" asks Maddie. "Are you sure?"

"She watches us all the time," Courtney says. "She even did it back when Beatrix visited here. Don't you remember when you joined our coven in Atlanta, Blackbird?"

"It's what Enora does," Mira says with a nod. "But it's getting much worse since Cordelia came here. Now it's virtually every night. It's because she's planning an attack. This is what she does before she strikes." Then Mira furrows her brow, and she stands up, searching the glade again. "She's watching us right now."

"Right now, Mira?" asks Maddie, sounding scared.

"Yes." Mira nods. "Reveal yourself, Panthera. *Revelare. Revelare.* Reveal your divination to the Hawthorne coven."

Mira's words echo around us, as if being broadcasted by speakers on the surrounding trees in the woods. I hear it repeated, seemingly louder and louder, amplified off the branches of trees in the surrounding dark woods.

"Reveal yourself. Revelare. Revelare."

I hear a gasp.

One of the girls screams.

And then, I feel her presence before I see it. The flames of our bonfire rise three times higher, heating my face. In the center of our bonfire is a fiery red-and-yellow form. It's a woman wearing a dress with a lace collar. Her body flickers inside the fire. I recognize Enora's hideously pretty face. But she's not turned toward me, she's staring down at Mira and Kenosha.

"Bravo, Raven," Enora says. "Bravo. Impressive." Her voice is broken up, as if broken up by the flames. "I see your magic is improving, thanks to my tutelage. You might even be besting good ole weeping willow over here."

"*You have no business watching us!*" Kenosha cries, jumping up.

"Oh, on the contrary, *council leader*, I was initiated by Falconsong in this very circle," Enora says. "With Bryce. Remember, Cadence? This is my coven. And aren't you and all Katie's friends, my *friends*? Actually, I was a little offended I wasn't invited." And the bitch-witch cackles; her laughter crackles and pops as if broken by fire. "Anyway, as usual, I heard little Katie wants to relinquish her magic and just go study. *After* she's done tormenting the fuck out of me."

"I've done nothing to you, Enora!" I shout.

"There's no other witch but Mud that could be casting," Enora says, shaking her head. "You know this well enough, *council members*. I taught Cadence how to dream cast."

"You were thrown out of this coven," Mira cries, shaking her head. She looks through Enora's body, in the flames, at me. "High Priestess, she's revealed her scrying! Simply demand she leaves. She's using our fire to scry. This is your grounds, not hers!"

I nod. But then, in the fiery red-and-yellow flames, Enora spins around and faces me. I lurch back. Her body, made up of flames, is terrifying.

"Nuh-uh-uh, Katie. Aren't you my friend? I haven't hurt you. *Yet*. I simply wanted to join your meeting and add my two cents to your circle."

Her eyes narrow and she glares at me. Then, through the flames, she raises her scarred right hand. Amid her flaming body, it looks weird. This is the hand I once burned.

"Consider this a final warning, my dear Amica. I won't attack if you stop. But if you don't back the fuck off from me and my friends, I'll be forced to cast the same magic as you to every witch in this circle, including—yes, Mira—this new litter. It's a simple request. Back the fuck off. Consider my warning a favor for what you did for me in Alabama. I don't forget when someone does me a favor, Cadence, but, if I were you, I wouldn't forget that I'm far better at dream casting than you. I already made your afterlife a hell. But I can work on here and now, if you prefer."

Then the flames explode. And with the explosion, the bitch's laughter echoes among the trees.

The bonfire quickly descends to a small crackle as before.

None of us says a word.

The newbies are, of course, completely freaked out. Many have turned away from the fire as if even looking at it will make that bitch reappear. I even hear whimpering—I think from shy Nancy.

A gentle breeze brushes my face amid the kindling. It's calm outside again.

"Well, that's...witchcraft, guys," Maddie quips.

"How long has she been spying on us?" Bryce asks Mira.

"Since Alondra cast her out of the coven, the council surmises," Mira says. "It's all she does, Bryce. But I've watched it increase with us since Adder cropped up."

"Her favorite thing is spying," adds Courtney. "I witnessed rituals—" She pauses, looks over at the new recruits. "Sacrifices made just to enhance her divination power. Panthera monitors everyone she hates. Like she did with you once, Cadence, when she took Mira and you helped Beatrix."

"Cadence," Kenosha says. "Are you certain you're not dream casting against her? Or even preparing any spells naming her or her coven?"

"I'm not attacking her, Kenosha," I say, shaking my head. "I don't even know why she's accusing me. I'm not aware of having done anything to her."

"The Council accepts," Mira says. But then she shakes her head. "But she's not convinced." Mira turns to each new recruit: Abella, Nancy, Beth, Noori, and Gail. "Welcome to Windstorm's Hawthorne coven. Consider yourselves initiated."

Poor Nancy puts her head in her hands and cries harder. Beth has an arm around her, comforting her.

"That was the coolest thing I've ever seen," Abella says with wide eyes.

8

OKAY

It feels so weird walking in line in the college dining commons holding a plastic tray. I am following my brother, and we're in line with all these kids. It's weird but fun. It's Taco Tuesday. My brother, Damien, now a Junior, invited me. The place is packed. A lot of students eat off campus later in the year, after they meet up with friends, but this is their first week of school. The TVs are gone. Two years ago they played cartoons and music videos on sets hanging from the walls. Now I suppose they figure everybody just checks their phones. And that's what everybody's doing right now. Their heads are lowered, staring at their cellphones.

"Hi, Damie," says a young blond girl in a skirt. She has a sultry grin and is carrying a tray. My brother's cute, you know. He's tall, handsome, with long hair hanging from one side, like a total surfer.

"Hey," Damie replies, all cool.

"Who's that?" I probe. I start spooning shredded beef onto the plate on my tray.

"Carla."

"Carla, huh? She likes you. I can tell. I never understood why a good-looking guy like you didn't take your time to meet other girls before latching on to my best friend."

"Your best friend is pretty good-looking herself, Cadence."

"Gross, Damien. Just stop."

"Hey, I didn't bring it up."

After I've got lettuce, beans, shredded beef, and a little red salsa slathered on taco shells, and a full glass with ice and Coke —oh, and two freshly baked chocolate chip cookies—I follow my brother to find a table. That's no easy feat. At a far corner in the hall, we sit down at a small yellow plastic table with two blood-orange plastic chairs.

"Hey, Damien," says a boy carrying a tray. "Hi, Ms. Wallace."

And then I partake in what I've been looking forward to all week, since my brother told me about this dinner. Taco Tuesday. I loved the idea of meeting Damie, not just for memories, but for Taco Tuesday. Tacos are the best food here at Hawthorne, you know. And...here goes...*umm*, that crunchy taste never disappoints.

"So, sis, you think Enora is up to her nasty tricks again?" Damie says. "I heard you saw her in ceremony. Maybe Enora conjured Escoba? Or was it Melanie? Didn't you say Melanie conjured the past once?"

"Maybe," I say with a shrug. "Or maybe I did? I don't know."

"But Enora wants to hurt us. All the sisters keep talking about it."

"Enora is Enora. I don't mind her so much anymore, Damie. I mean, I still think she's a disgusting, filthy, murdering bitch, but I have a better understanding of her."

Damie looks up from his soft taco and furrows his brow. I laugh. "She tried to murder Bryce and bleed you to death."

Well, he has a point there.

I bite into more taco. And it tastes sooo good! But, you know, there's a little bit of sadness in this culinary delight. I don't tell my brother, but that taste of shredded beef mixed with cheddar cheese in a crunchy shell makes me think about my college dorm years and how they're over. Look, the tacos aren't *that* good, but it's the memory of it. That memory is priceless.

"I know Enora's a monster, Damie," I say, after another swallow. Then I wipe my mouth on a napkin. Some of my black lipstick bleeds on the paper. I lift my finger, crunching a little more taco shell first, and then say, "You can never trust her because she only thinks of herself. But that makes her less frightening and very predictable. I feel like I understand her loathsome self better than I ever did before."

"After you shared her black magic?"

"No, after I spent time with her. And after I felt like she wasn't all that different from myself. You're right, we both practice dark magic now."

I bite into a cookie over that. That makes me smile. See, that's what you can do when you're an adult in college. You can bite into a cookie. I could have just eaten an entire platter full of cookies if I wanted to. That's why college is so special. You can't do that when you're back home with your mom and dad. I remember all those times spent here with Maddie, laughing hysterically over who-knows-or-cares-what-the-hell-what when she and I ate together every day as Freshmen. College is the first time you're totally free. Do you get what I mean?

"Cordelia showed up accusing me of attacking her and her friends," I say. "That's not evil. Maddie or I would have done precisely the same thing to her coven if I thought Enora was attacking us. But it totally freaked out the newbies."

"Are you attacking her?"

"No." At least, I don't think I am.

"What about Escoba? You don't think seeing our ancestor was Enora's doing?"

"Enora. Escoba. Let's just not talk about it right now, Damie, okay?"

Then, thankfully, he agrees. Honestly, I don't want to discuss witches. But maybe that's why he wanted to meet?

So I eat. I watch him and others around us doing that. So many students are sitting alone staring at their cellphones and eating delicious tacos. It's fantastic and I love it.

"We don't have to talk about witches," he says with a shrug after a long silence.

"Then what'd you want to tell me? What was so important that you wanted to meet? 'Fess up, Damien. Hmm? Maybe... perhaps something about my best friend and *you*? *Hmm?*"

He glances at his phone and then stuffs it back in his pants pocket. He shakes his head. Then he freaks me out by pushing his plate away.

"Sis, we all decided that I should be the one to tell you this."

"What? Oh, God, Damie, what the hell is the matter? Is someone sick? Is something wrong with Maddie?"

"No," he says with a chuckle. "It's not Madison. Or—" He furrows his brow again and stares at the table. "It sort of is. It's about all of us. Maddie and I decided it'd be better if I tell you. I mean, you've freaked out Maddie enough that she's worried you'll cast a spell and throw her in the hospital if she tells you. Dad and her mom wanted to do it, but we had sort of a family meeting. Everyone was willing to tell you, but they all voted for me to actually do it."

"To do what?"

"Because, you know, Dad always teases that you treat me like a son. The family thinks I can get away with things much better than anyone around you and—"

"What is it, Damie!" I say, hitting the table. "Shit. Stop it! What the hell's going on?"

"Dad's getting married."

"What?"

"Dad's...getting...married," he drawls slowly. Then he laughs nervously. "God, I don't even think *I* can tell you. I'm scared of you myself."

I realize I'm just staring with my mouth gaping open. Because I don't think I understand what the hell he's saying. I mean, I heard the words, it's just not registering. What did he say?

"What do you mean? *Married?* Dad just lost Mom."

"He's in love. Just like...well...he's in love. So he wanted to tell you, but with what happened after you heard about Madds and me, we all got together and thought about the best way to tell you. They all thought I should do it. Everyone was willing to tell, but they thought I should bring it up. So, sis, what I'm trying to tell you is—"

"Dad's marrying Aunt Jane?"

"Yeeaaah." And he stares down at the table.

"Jane and Dad? Aunt Jane? My best friend Madison's mom, Aunt Jane, is marrying our dad? They're getting married together?"

"Yeah."

"Why?"

"They're in love."

"Mom just died."

"Mom died five years ago, Cadence."

I look around again. There are so many small tables occupied by lonely kids. That's kind of sad. I met Maddie at orientation, and I was never alone like that in college. I guess I never thought about how lucky I was back then. We never appreciate anything until it's too late.

"You all right, sis?"

No. Not really. But I nod.

"You're not going to, you know, go berserko and blow something up?"

"What?" I laugh. Then I drink some Coke through a straw and shake my head. "No."

"Okay, Damie."

"Okay?... Okay, what?"

I look up at my brother and nod slowly. "Okay."

He takes a deep breath and leans back in his chair and nods too. "Okay."

"But they just met."

He drinks some Coke through a straw too and runs his hand through his hair.

"They were getting close even back on Thanksgiving," he says. "Remember our Thanksgiving two years ago when Maddie went crazy and we left? They already liked each other back then. They're planning a ceremony at Hawthorne Church. It'll be in a couple months. Of course, if you're for it, Aunt Jane and Maddie want you to be one of Jane's bridesmaids. Jane's agreed to make it a fully Christian wedding for Dad. No pagan stuff. They're going to get married by a priest. But Bryce came up with the idea of having the reception at your house after. I think if Dad weren't so averse to our witchcraft, he'd get married in the backyard, like you and Bryce. Again, Cadence, they would have told you in person, but last year was so hard on you, they thought I should be the one to spill the beans."

"It's just so weird. I was prepared for you to tell me something about Maddie and you. But *Dad*?"

"Well, actually, Maddie and I—"

"Stop," I say, putting up a hand. "Just stop there. One thing at a time."

"Sure," he says with a chuckle. "Never mind."

"Okay," I drawl again.

"Okay?" he asks with a nod and a smile.

"Sure. Okay."

"I really think Mom would have liked Jane," Damie says, biting into a cookie. "Did they ever meet?"

"Yeah. The first-day orientation in our dorm room. Jane and Mom are the sweetest women in the world, you know. Sweeter than me, for sure. But, no, they never got to know each other well. It's too bad. I'm sure they would have hit it off well."

I look down. But now I've lost my appetite. I don't feel mad. Or do I? No, I feel kind of numb. But being numb is bad because I was feeling good earlier, reminiscing about the dining commons. Dark magic has always made me feel numb, and I don't want to feel that void anymore. It's lonely. Maybe I want to be alone? Or maybe, actually, I am getting angry?

"How's the baby?" Damie asks. "You still getting morning sickness?"

I smile and touch my belly. Then I shake my head. "Not so much anymore. But no kicking or large stomach yet."

"Are you going to be Aunt Jane's bridesmaid?" he asks sincerely.

"I don't know," I say with a sigh. "It's so weird, Damien. Between you, Maddie, and now her mom...like, why can't you guys just find other people to be with?"

"You're our High Priestess and leader," Damie says with a shrug.

"It's just so weird."

"No weirder than Hawthorne."

"Well, I warned you about Hawthorne. Okay." I lift my Coke glass in a toast. "To family. To Mom and Dad. To Maddie. Ugh, you and Maddie. To our mom in the Summerland. I really think Mom would have loved you and Maddie together. And, yeah, she would have loved Aunt Jane."

"Thanks, sis," he says, raising his soda glass. "This means a lot to us."

"Thank you. Wow, Taco Tuesday at Hawthorne dining commons again, huh?" I heave a sigh and look around again at all the students. Many have books on their tables and are studying. "This place has so many good memories. I love it."

"You can come again next week. I can give you the card. Harvey probably wouldn't even mind if you stay over at our dorm next week. He's off traveling for a regatta meet in Austin. And, you know, I'm almost always at Maddie's place anyway." Then he puts a finger to his lips. "Just don't tell Dad."

"Don't you think he already knows?"

9
———

ALU

I'M LOOKING AT THE RAIN THROUGH A LARGE HOLE IN THE WALL ON the summit of a hilltop in the wilderness. A damp tape-and-paper border surrounds a large rectangular opening. Spruce walls with a few stray red painted symbols and lines surround the shelter. I smell the wood mixed with the dank leaves and grass. The rain's pouring so hard it is a solid sheet of water before my face, collecting into pools all over the muddy grass. The rain pelts branches and leaves, shaking and swaying tall trees over the trail meandering deeper into a dense thicket below. I'm shivering, without clothes, standing perfectly still on icy cement, holding a single candle by my chest. I keep blinking and, although I have a roof over my head, the water keeps pelting my eyes. The candle by my chest struggles to remain lit, and I feel as if it *has to* keep burning. As if, if it's snuffed out, not only will it leave me, *I'll* leave me.

In the far distance, amid the roar of rain, I hear screaming. A moment ago I was watching a lady in a black robe, crouched on my patio, yelling. Then I couldn't hear her. Now I can't see her. It was Escoba Hawthorne. She seemed so intense, as if in either physical or mental anguish.

Goety, goety, goety.

"Hand me the candle, Cadence," Bryce says.

"Are you a member of Psi Kappa Psi?"

"I was. Before I graduated. I'm an honoree."

"I didn't know I'd ever get to meet an *honoree.*"

"That window over there. It's lit up every night by a ghost. And it's not Escoba who haunts that window. It's Alondra."

"*Prohibe,*" I say, shaking my head. I close my eyes and concentrate so hard with all my magical intent. "*Prohibe.* Stop this. I know it's you, Enora! Stop it! Hawthorne is my hallowed ground!"

"Forfeit your candle and you pass away."

My candle snuffs out.

Surgi! Surgi! Evigilare faciati. Prohibe. Evigilare faciati.

The rectangular hole in the wall before me is large enough to climb through. So I do. I climb outside. But then I'm met with a tempest, and I'm thrown down on my knees in the mud. I shiver, wrapping my arms around my bare skin. It's so cold! And... My god, I've lost my candle!

I turn.

I can't return to my shelter. The hole in the wall I was staring through is now solid glass.

"*Surgi! Surgi!*"

I'm running.

Around the building, I'm searching for warmth. It is in ruins. Sections of the building rise to two, even three stories, with metal scaffolding, but only the first floor is intact. I find a purple bonfire at the center of a backyard full of wild grass. Despite this horrible downpour, the violet bonfire in the field stays lit. This wild grass amid the forest reminds me of home.

"Blessed Hecate!" I cry to the clouds. "Wake me from this wandering! Shine down and awaken me. I am the Hawthorne Witch. You hold no power here, Enora!"

But am I asleep? If this is a dream, it doesn't matter if it's my hallowed grounds. She can do whatever she wants to me. Or am I in a witch wandering?

My bare feet slap and slush through muddy pools of water as I run around the side of the building. There has to be another way back in. There just has to be. I'm so cold.

Not finding anything, I rush back to the violet flame. Then I crouch over the fire, shaking like crazy, running my hands over it for warmth. But, like my violet bonfire back home, there's no warmth.

Down in the logs between flickering purple flames, I discover a burning pair of jeans and a dress. This is...Bryce's pair of pants. How? Why? I recall buying him the pants when we went shopping in a mall in Savannah, but I don't know whose dress this is beside it. The dress seems to be hundreds of years old.

Revelare. Revelare.

Goety. Goety. Goety.

I blink like crazy in the rain, my eyes becoming wetter. I remember this pyre now. She put the clothes in the fire to hide the evidence. She had his clothes, and she had to get rid of them, so she took them to my bonfire and tried to burn them. She couldn't have known I'd be preparing my own rites tonight. Maybe that's why Enora's casting this dream spell on me? Enora sent Cordelia. Now, Enora's finally done it. See, she's not only planning to haunt my coven's dreams again. Judging from the evidence in the flames, she is doing something far worse. *She's having an affair with Bryce!*

The trees sway, but it isn't the storm, it's *my* storm. *My* windstorm.

How could Bryce do this to me!

It's been hard, and he's always working, but we still love each other. Don't we?

Some animal touches my leg. It feels sticky and slimy.

I whirl around. Then I lurch back.

Under me, a small ashen-white creature crouches. It's about the height of my knees. His face and skin are pale and wrinkly. But, worse, lanky black creatures tower above us. Tall creatures, like trees in the forest, with no arms, no mouths, no discernible faces, just demons with white eyes, shining down at me. And there's a rotten smell. It smells musty and rancid, like a dead animal.

I hear screaming again.

The white goblin lunges at me, throwing me on my back. Then it sits on top of my chest. His head snaps back and forth. He gazes up at the towering dark devils. Then he looks down at me with blinking dark eyes. I expect a sinister smile, but he has no ears or mouth.

I traipse down a busy narrow hall with necklaces, scarfs, and beads hanging from the ceiling. It still smells damp and woodsy from the pouring rain, but it's nice under a shelter—even a small shelter like this one. I have to duck under the strings of low-hanging beads. The beads would have knocked the bonnet from my head if it weren't tied around my neck.

It is one of my favorite bonnets. My mother made it for me when I was a girl, and I still wear it, even now that I'm older. Looking down I see my lovely long blue dress with a white ruffled collar. My dress, though pretty, feels a little stifling tonight.

Tables are covered with all these silver trinkets, rubies and emeralds, crystals, and wooden crosses. A few tables have bones and skulls—like real skulls. One dirty skull is really big with horns. And beside that are a few human skulls. Sticks tied together in the shape of five-pointed stars are leaning against the wall. And cards and gems are laid out over a black mat. And there's such a wonderful smell of incense everywhere—it's frankincense mixed with lavender amid the dust. Candles are lit. The candles are our main source of light. I don't see any lamps.

Essie's laughing. She is always so cheery and I love her.

Essie's a dark-skinned woman, a slave on the farm. She's wearing a white headdress and a long white dress. She already commented how she shouldn't be seen here with a woman of such station as myself. I told her to stop being silly. I mean, we're both witches.

I love this place. It's so magical. I let Essie and her friends do what they will in secret here, and she gets lots of visitors. I stay mum, just as I'm mum about my sisters Emma and Janus.

She leads me slowly by each table, her fingers, covered in shiny brass rings, touching various objects. She lifts them before her eyes, inspecting them. She smells a few, or just runs her fingers along them. Shaking her head, she returns most to the tables. Only a select few are handed to me. She instructed me to put the ones she picks in a wicker basket that I'm carrying over my shoulder.

"This," she says. "And this. No, not this, Abbie. But this. Yes, oh yes, this will do really good. You have his lock of hair? I hope you remembered the lock. It's most important for the pot."

"Yes," I say. "But you're sure your root work will work, Escoba?"

"It sure will." She puts some small bones in a bowl and nods. "Sure will." They look like chicken bones. "Misses, don't worry. You gather the things and I'll cook something up for your bag. I will make you the gris-gris. But, you know, it could bloody well kill 'em. Is that what you want? I've come to like master."

"Goddamned fool deserves it," I say, shaking my head. "I hate him. I hate him so much now. Found the garment outside in the yard by our logs. I caught him trying to burn it with his pants. Can you believe that? I know he's been out fucking. You use your Vodun and take care of him, Essie, and there'll be a great reward. Promise."

"Repay me, yes," she says, turning back gravely. She forces a smile. "You and me are friends, right? Friends? I have charms you don't know 'bout in master's farm that'll take care of him and that hussy. But no Vodun. It's true I might have been born Haitian, but I practice Hoodoo under Jesus, misses. I told you. Learned and used power in Congo Square. I'm Christian like you, misses, not Vodun. Christian."

"Sure, Essie," I say, touching her arm. "Sure."

I lift a jar full of eyeballs. "What's this? Eye of newt?" I chuckle. "Should we use wool of bat and dog tongues?"

"What'cha sayin'!" Escoba furrows her brow and bursts into laughter. "Umble-cum-stumble." She picks up a bunch of stones then shakes her head. "You're crazy, Abbie. You've always been crazy. Well, we're almost done. There is great magic in opal. See the dark shade? Get some of those stones, you hear, Abbie? And rubies to represent blood. Onyx for our craft, like your robes, and we cast dark reflections. Your spell and mine, we bring them magic. And plain stone and grave dirt. We need grit along with that lock of hair. Then, we cook them together. We put it all together, we're gonna bring over bull parts and them stones and grit, and cook them all in a stew. Fire will spark and burn them all in my pot, just like we're gonna burn whoever dared make love to your man for you. She's gonna pay, I tell you. She'll pay, Abbie. Both of them will pay good."

I nod and throw some rocks angrily into my open basket.

"But you know, Abbie," Escoba says, stopping for a moment. She turns and gazes right into my eyes, looking a little sad. "Another way is to just give this time. You and I are friends. Yes? Sometimes...sometimes, misses, it is better off just giving things time. I know it hurts, but sometimes it wasn't intended by the strumpet. Sometimes love messes with the mind. Anyway, time will let you see who your husband is playing around with soon enough. Doesn't have to be by moon magic. It can be without magic at all. That's what I think you should do. I told you, I'd give it time and not cast any spells."

"No, I want to take care of them," I say, narrowing my eyes and vehemently shaking my head. "I have to, Essie. I already told you, I laid some curses down myself, but I need your gris-gris. I need your root work. I'm done with Bryce, I tell you. I'm done. I need you to finish Enora and Bryce once and for all. I know they were together, hiding sin in the fire back home. Can't you do it, Escoba? For Hawthorne? Or not?"

Escoba stops her work and smiles ruefully. Then she puts a hand on each of my shoulders and nods. "Bairn, bairn, Cadence. Bairn, bairn."

I'm running through bushes, stepping over branches, and tripping over more muddy holes in the uneven ground. I think I've stabbed the sole of my foot a couple times. It could be bleeding. I don't care. I can't care. I'm just so upset.

How could Bryce do this to me!

But the storm is calming. It's just drizzling.

I'm hardly calm inside. The storm still rages inside me.

I'm so mad! So furious. How could he do this again? *Bryce and Enora! Why?* What does he see in that horrible bitch? But... I'm awake. I mean, I'm freezing, so I must be awake. I think this is a wandering. How can it not be? I'm naked, freezing, and totally crazy.

I have to find shelter.

Enora must have cursed me. But if Enora cast this spell, my incantation commanding the dream to stop should have stopped it? Maybe it did? Maybe Enora intended to do something even more horrible?

But why would Bryce be with Enora!

Wait... It wasn't Enora and Bryce, was it? It was Escoba and Josiah. What am I thinking. I'm not Abigail. I'm Cadence.

The half moon and stars shining above light surrounding trees. It's bright enough for the tall thin trees to cast shadows over the muddy trail I'm rushing along. I haven't seen one street, not even a streetlight. That's so weird. No matter where you wander in Hawthorne Forest, you always see a building with yellow light lurking around a corner. Unless I wandered too far?

I shake, not only from cold, but from sudden fear. Chandra! God, Chandra, what about my baby! I have to get shelter, I just have to, not for me but for you, darling.

A path widens into a larger dirt road. And...there it is! I see my house in the far distance up the hillside. But maybe the storm knocked out the power. It's so dark along our driveway. The electricity was on the fritz a couple years ago. Maybe there's something wrong with the wiring in our old house again?

But, no, I don't see cars either. In fact, wait, I don't even see Alondra's old decorative red carriage. No... Stranger, there's no pavement in the driveway, and the house is missing all the plants I grew on our front porch.

I slow down, walking barefoot over the wet rocks and mud. Then I approach my front door. But, of course, I'm not carrying keys. At least I'm under the shelter of our patio now.

I knock hard. Nothing...so I try again.

Come on Bryce, open up!

What if Bryce doesn't hear me? God, what if he's working really late in one of the offices in our history building?

I pound the door some more.

The door creaks open slightly. A tall brown-skinned man I've never seen is on the threshold wearing a long white night-gown and cap and holding an old lit oil lamp. He's dressed so weird. But his eyes seem familiar.

"Loose woman!" he exclaims, opening his eyes wide. "What are you doing out in the middle of the night? Where are your clothes?"

"Let me in. This is my house!"

"*Your* house? It's not your house. It's...wait, I thought you left us? *Come here to kill me too, sorceress!*"

He tries to slam the door on me, but I'm desperate. I stop the door with my leg. I just have to get in. I heave as hard as I can, but he's blocking me with his body.

"I just want to get in!" I cry. "Come on! Open the door!"

"Maverick, who's that by the door?" asks a woman's voice.

Maverick? Maverick? Maverick is my great-great-ancestor, Escoba's son. I'm scared. No...sick. This is the past. My ancestors' past. I'm home, just...two hundred years in the past.

He slams the door in my face.

"*Surgi,*" I say sluggishly. "*Surgi.* Please. Stop this. *Surgi. Evigilare faciati. End this spell now.*"

"You spellcasting!" he cries, throwing the door open again. "Cursing me? You get the hell out of here, witch! No one's gonna put a spell on me. Momma died from all that mumbo jumbo. If you don't leave, I'll get the watchman. You're in Hawthorne. Now get away from here, you hag!"

And he slams the door on my face again.

I feel so sick. And then... I'm falling...

10

SHELTER

"Cadence!" Bryce asks. "Oh, God, Cadence! Are you all right?"

I hear him, but my eyes are closed. I don't want to open them.

"Cadence!" he asks, shaking me. "Cadence, what's happening? You disappeared from bed."

My teeth are chattering. My whole body is shaking. I open my eyes and Bryce is looking down at me. Holding me. I see our crystal chandelier behind him, but it's not glistening. It's too dark with all the lights out. Only our streetlamps outside are lighting the entryway behind me. The chandelier above is a little out of focus. Bryce is brushing my drenched hair from my eyes.

"What happened, baby?" he asks quietly. "What's going on, Cadence? You're so cold."

"I don't know."

"Enora?"

"Maybe. My eyes were open, Bryce. But I was sleeping...I think. I must have been."

"Can you get up?"

"No."

No... I feel real sick. My heart's racing. I'm afraid.

I was seeing the past? Why? How?

"Get me a bucket, Bryce. Quick."

He lets my head down gently on our hard floor and rushes to another room. I lean over on my side, doing everything I can to not throw up. Then he hands me a bowl and drapes a blanket over me. I lean over the bowl.

But I don't throw up. I do everything I can not to. I hate throwing up.

"God, Cadence, our baby." He rubs my hands. "You can't be out like this—"

"Don't you think I know that?"

I lean on my elbow. He just kneels beside me. He looks worried, so I frown.

"Sorry," I say. "I was at the Billington House, I think. But half of me was seeing my past. No, not seeing the past, I was actually *in the past*. And I was terrified that I'd be trapped there."

"Was it Enora?"

I don't answer. I just listen to the rain.

Just like at the Billington House, the rain is rushing down like a wall of water outside our front patio. Just in time, I suppose, because now I'm under shelter.

"God, Cadence," he says, and he puts his arms around me and holds me. "And your skin is so cold."

"I saw some sort of goblin," I say. "A small, faceless creature I had never seen before. I felt like he was casting this nightmare on me. Maybe it was the creature, not Enora?"

"What kind of creature?"

"A short creature without a face. Just eyes."

"An Alu?"

"Huh?" I ask with a chuckle, looking at his eyes. "Maybe. Whatever, professor. Surrounding that small monster were all these horrifying dark demon creatures, standing over us. No, I felt like it was cast by them, or the small creature, not Enora. I don't think it was Enora. But I don't know."

"Alus appear in dreams. They're demons that haunt our sleep. Maybe Enora summoned one? But you were outside. You were awake. I don't get it."

"Maybe I was sleeping *and* wandering? I couldn't really have been in the past, could I? Maybe in this weird witch town I could? Can I travel in time now? As if witchcraft weren't fucking weird enough. But...I told you, I was at the Billington House. And...I saw Escoba, Abigail, and Maverick. An older Maverick. And, no, I was Abigail I think, Bryce. But the Billington House is under construction, right? You told me they have the first floor done?" He nods. "That's where I was. The Billington House. But then I saw Maverick by our front door. He greeted me, not like the little boy I used to see as a ghost around our college, but as the adult who probably built this town. Remember how after Escoba died, people in town say Abigail roamed the town, lost in madness? That's what I was doing. Maverick acted like I was Abigail. I even had a vision of Escoba fixing up that brew she gave Abigail to kill Josiah after Abigail found out he had cheated on her."

He nods, but he doesn't look very interested. He just looks worried.

"Abigail and Escoba were friends, Bryce," I say. "Did you know that?"

"The story goes that Abigail met with Escoba for the first time for the spell. I always thought they didn't know each other well until she came to curse her husband."

"No, they knew each other very well. They were good friends. Slave and enslaver, but friends. And both were witches, even before Enora cast her curse. It makes the story so much more tragic."

"Cadence, forget about all this. Let me help you get upstairs so you can go shower."

"I was mixing up Escoba and Josiah with you," I say, shaking my head. "God, I kept thinking you were messing around with Enora." I pull away from his embrace. "Have you been? Tell me the truth, Bryce. Are you cheating on me with Enora?"

"What? Of course not! Babe, you're pregnant and you're wandering with our baby. You can't be out in the cold."

"Don't you think I know that!"

Fuck! I love him, but he can be so annoying. Especially when he starts hanging with Escoba again.

"I can't call the cops every time you leave," he snaps.

"You're always just concerned about yourself," I say. Then I look down the dark hallway. "What time is it, anyway?"

I stand up. I'm not shivering anymore. I feel warm. I'm not even dizzy. But my long hair and bare skin are still dripping wet.

I let the blanket fall. Then I gaze down at him, still lying on his side on the floor. It's evening outside but with the outdoor lights on, despite the downpour, it's a bit brighter than inside. Inside, there is only a distant light upstairs, probably from our bedroom. And right now, the outdoor light is shining over his bushy eyebrows, hard jawline, and amazing blue eyes.

"I really love you. But you worry too much about me."

The rain is pouring so hard that I can't see much beyond the porch outside. It's like a veil of water again. It's like that wall of rain that stood before me when I held my candle in the Billington House.

"In my vision..." I continue staring outside. "I saw Josiah's clothes in a bonfire in the Billington House backyard with a dress. I think Escoba or Josiah was trying to hide the clothes from Abigail after they had that sexual encounter on Hilltop Bluff. Abigail discovered it in the past, and in my confused mind, I thought it was you and Enora. In my mind, I thought you were cheating on me, being with Enora again. But—" I shake my head, looking down at him again. "I know you would never do that. Right? You're not, right? We love each other too much. You're not having an affair with Enora?"

He doesn't answer. I think he's annoyed I keep asking him.

He has such neat facial hair. That's his *professor look* for his students. He keeps it perfectly trimmed. It's so cute. And he always has a bit of dark stubble. I love that. But he's not in a suit or button-down now, like he wears during lectures. He's in his white T-shirt and pajama pants.

I smell the damp fur of a deer crouched under bushes in a ditch about two hundred yards down the hill. She's waiting for the storm to clear. But she knows she's not far from a stag, which is by a nearby watering hole. They're all taking shelter under the trees from the rain. The stag's gotten large and is ready for rutting. After the rain stops, even as the water and mud still surround them, they intend to come together and mate among all the leaves and mud. That's so arousing. But despite my vision of twigs and mud, here by our door it smells nice and clean from all the water washing away the earth. I love the smell of fresh rain.

And now, here in the cleanness of our foyer, though Bryce showered, I smell a slight remnant of his cologne too. His woodsy smell mixes with the fresh water collecting on our cement driveway and front garden. It arouses me. He knows I love his cologne. He might have washed it away before he went to bed, but I still smell him.

I see birds hiding under thrush, also trying to keep dry. I never noticed before how much rain can affect animals.

I stand by the door just gazing out at our front yard.

"Your mascara is running," he says, tearing his eyes away. "Your face looks different than before, Katie."

"Hmm, I'm wearing makeup?" I ask, turning back. "Weird. I remember taking it off before I went to bed. But I'm feeling warm now, Bryce. I feel so much better. I'm more worried about you."

I fold my arms and lean on the frame of the open door with no wish to close it. I love the sound of the rain trickling from the roof and through our gutters onto the ground. I gaze at our replica red carriage. It's ironic that such an old thing comforts me, reminding me that I'm in the twenty-first century now, not in my ancestors' past. Half of me wants to drift back outside and sit naked on the carriage watching the downpour, or maybe get Bryce to come outside with me? I could...perhaps, sit on his lap? We could stare out from under the shelter as the rain crashes down on my flower garden?

I laugh. Then I shake some of the water from my hair. Some of the drops from my hair hit Bryce's face, and he has to brush the water from his eyes. *Oops.*

"You remember going to sleep?" he asks.

"Uh huh."

"Close the door, Cadence," Bryce says. "It's cold outside and wet."

"No, I like it open. It smells so nice and fresh. I like it. Just as I like the drops falling on my naked skin. Right, Bryce?"

"Your makeup isn't dark," he says, squinting up at me. "It's weird. You're wearing red lipstick and blush. You look totally different than I've ever seen you before. I've never seen you wear that color."

"Do you like it?"

"No."

"Really?" I ask with a chuckle and a shrug. "Fine. Guess I won't wear it like that ever again."

"No," he says, shaking his head. "That's not what I mean. I mean *no.*"

"My hair probably looks like a total mess from all the rain."

"No, I mean *no*, Cadence." He's looking very stern. Then he wags his finger. "*No.*"

"What do you mean, *no*?" I ask with a laugh. "Fine, it wasn't the rain and I don't look good in this makeup."

"No, Cadence, I mean no, we're not making love after you just left the house and stood in the rain naked for hours under Enora's curse. No sex this time after your witch wandering. It's not right. We need to figure out what the hell's happening to you."

"Who said anything about sex?" I ask with a laugh.

"Let me help you upstairs for a warm shower."

"A warm shower would sure feel nice," I say with a nod. Especially with him in the shower beside me, soaping and rubbing my back...

"You're feeling better?"

"I feel wonderful."

I do. I wipe water off my forehead again. Then I stretch my arms, by the door, leaning over him. Some of the water from my skin falls on him again, I think. This time, he doesn't bother to brush the water away. He just stares at my body.

The rainfall is calming. My naked body must be quite visible from the hillside. It feels inappropriate in front of my house, but I doubt anyone is going to be wandering around the neighborhood at this time, in this weather. There are a lot of witches in Hawthorne, but it's unlikely they'll be wandering on this exact hillside tonight.

"Actually, I feel warm."

"No, I said."

I stare down at him. Then I lick my lips. I feel feral. Like the deer in their shelter. And now it's not raining so hard. And, you know. I just... So... I don't know...

He slowly shakes his head.

The doe is still crouched in the bushes, with the stag nearby. I smell their wet fur in the leaves. And the stag's horns. The fur mixed with that earthen smell is so erotic, as if they're naked because of the rainstorm too.

"I want to fuck you."

He shakes his head.

I crouch down slowly, so carefully, touching his hair and face gently with my fingers, as if I'm hypnotizing him. Then I'm probing under his T-shirt. Am I casting a spell on him? Or is a spell being cast on both of us? I want him. I want to touch him. I want to feel him. I want to embrace him. I love him so much, I want to...devour him. Like an animal. I mean, what can I say, I want to fuck him.

But right now, I'm actually just content sending kisses down his neck.

"Cadence, I said no," he says. But he laughs, because I'm all over him. "Wanderings make you do this. It's not right. You scared me. You can't just ignore that and kiss me."

"You're gonna make such an amazing dad, Bryce," I say, running my hand outside his white cotton shirt and pants. I like even just stroking his clothes, knowing what lies underneath. "You're so authoritative. You're going to—" I kiss his lips again. "Make up for me being such a witch."

"You're not that kind of witch."

"Sweet...but, no." I push his nose with my finger. Then I slowly stroke the thin hairs on his cheek. "I kinda am. You know, Enora made me wicked."

I lick his neck with my tongue again.

Then I bite his neck.

"*Ow!*" he exclaims, pushing me from him. "Shit, Cadence! What the hell was that! Just go upstairs."

"Let's make love, Bryce. Right by the door. You were right. I really want to have sex. Sorry, I want to make love with you. Let's just do it by the front door. Or...we can go outside on the patio? Don't you want to?"

"Yes... But not after what happened, babe."

"I'm in the mood, hun. Come on." He laughs. I think that sounded really whiny. In the shadows, I catch him fighting a smile. "It must have been a wandering. I feel so attracted to you right now. Why don't you ever have wanderings? I'd love to see my man walking in the forest naked and coming home ravenous for my body too."

"I'm glad you're feeling better," he says with a chuckle.

He tries to get up, but I don't let him. I lick his neck and face again, and then send more kisses along his face. I'm all over him. Then we're smooching again.

"Look, Cadence," he says, backing up. "You freaked me out. You even nearly threw up. We don't know if Enora's attacking you. You should—"

But our lips touch again. And he pulls me closer. I think it's a battle, you know. His paternal instinct versus his lover one. I'm trying to get the lover one to win out right now. I don't want to go up and shower. I want him to make love to me.

I press against his soft lips hard with mine as I hold him tight. Then I feel a hand wander along my side, stroking the curve of my damp naked breast. He brushes his fingers across my nipple. And then he runs another hand down over my ass.

My hand glides down below his waist. My fingers land on his bulge under his underwear. He might be saying he doesn't want to make love, but his cock is saying quite another thing. And then...

I shiver. My body ruins everything.

"*Get upstairs now, Cadence!*" he barks. I laugh when he lifts a finger like a dad again. "I mean it. You need to get warm. Think of our baby."

I think about how the door's still open. Even though nobody in their right mind would come walking by our house in the middle of the night in the pouring rain, I love that someone can. It's nasty that I'm in the nude licking and biting his neck, fondling him, just right out in the open.

I pull down his pants. His cock is long and hard. I push him gently against the wall, stroking his cock and running my fingers over his balls as my tongue enters his mouth again. I run my other hand along his cheek, over all that stubble I love.

"Take me," I whisper. "Fuck me, Bryce. You were right, as usual. You're always right. It was a wandering. So, that means… I really want to fuck you right now."

"Cadence—"

I fall to my side. Then Bryce, being the sweetest man in the world, reaches down to see if I'm okay. I knew he would. (*Shh.* That was my plan, okay? I am getting wicked, aren't I?)

He falls by my side. He's only in his shirt now. His pants are bunched down by his feet. Then I roll with him by the doorway, laughing.

"What about the baby?" he asks quietly between kisses. "I don't want to hurt her."

"Dr. Morey said sex wasn't a problem, Bryce."

"But the door is open."

"I love it. There are deer outside taking shelter in the rain. They're about halfway down the hill on the way to campus. The doe wants to have sex with the stag so bad. I can feel them, Bryce. Can you? Try to use your magic. See if you can see them or smell them like I can. They're waiting for just the right moment, like us—" I run my tongue along his. "They've been waiting for the rain to calm down, like it is now. Then they're going to get together under shelter, really close, and… I want to do that right now with you. I want to mate right by the door, like them, but while the rain falls outside."

And I'm on top of him. I've positioned him so that I'm already moving up and down on him.

The sex is wonderful. All that sickness has left me. But as I make love with him, half of him still seems to want to punish me by wagging a finger again. I wouldn't entirely mind. Maybe I want to be punished?

"Oh, Bryce," I say, feeling him inside me. "Everything is so hard. Why have we been so distant?"

That seems to stop his confusion. He finally takes me into his strong arms in a tight embrace.

"I love you, Cadence. And... I was so worried when you left the house. But I told you to stop doing this."

So I stop.

I *really, really* don't want to...but I do.

The last time I had a wandering like this and attacked him by our front door, we fought for weeks. It nearly broke up our relationship. That's the last thing I want right now. I don't think I could take losing Bryce.

But stopping kills me.

"I'm sorry," I say quietly with a nod, just lying on top of him in his embrace. "I really am sorry, Bryce."

He doesn't let me go. But he doesn't move either. Neither of us moves.

I just hear the rain. The water still smells fresh. Nice. It's clean and so nice, like being in Bryce's arms. And, though he doesn't want to make love, I don't want him to let me go. That's one thing I can't let him do.

"I'm sorry too," he says quietly, running his hand along my wet back, massaging me, and kissing my lips gently. "No matter what happens, school or witchcraft, I will always love you."

"Marriage is like a dance, you know," I say with a nod. "Lately we seem to be out of sync. But we still love each other?"

"Yes, Cadence," he says with a nod. "I love you."

And then we just hold each other.

But the weirdest thing is we're still intertwined. We're still together. Nobody's stopping a thing. We're pausing. Like our marriage. We're married but we're not. Now we're making love, but we're not. Do you understand? Sometimes I get deep, I suppose. I don't know. But, if you get what I'm trying to tell you, it kind of makes me want to cry.

Are things getting this bad between us? Maybe if I weren't pregnant, Bryce would leave me? My curse did make me a bitch a few months ago. I probably deserved it. Maybe it wasn't even the curse? God, maybe our marriage is dying? But I think all my dark magic is making me jaded—too dark to cry now.

So I don't.

"Just love me, Bryce," I whisper in his ear. "That's all I want."

He squeezes me tighter.

And then...we're moving again, so slowly and quietly this time. The rain is now just a light drizzle. The fury of my primal desire has left me. But I still love him *so* much.

He runs his hand along my wet back again. My skin is not as wet, but my hair is still drenched. I feel the cold wetness in my hair run over my cheeks as he runs his fingers through it. I kiss his cheek while moving my palm over his hair. He's so warm.

"Feel good, honey?" I whisper in his ear. "I just want you to feel good. Slow if you want, or fast. Whatever. Whatever, for you, Bryce. Just...let's not stop. I just want you to feel good. Is that wrong? But...I'm the one who's sorry. If it is my magic that makes you hold me, let me go. Only in love should we be together. That's all I've ever asked for. I really believe that."

"Katie, you just don't know how hard it is when you leave," Bryce whispers in my ear with a sigh. "That's why I'm mad."

"But you're always mad."

We both laugh.

"I'm doing everything I can to keep it together," he says quietly. "I told you before, you're not going crazy. I am. I get it, babe." And he moves a little again. "I do want you, Katie. I want you now. And I never want to let you go."

"Because of magic?"

"Because of love," he whispers softly in my ear.

And then I remember Josiah saying that. Escoba was unsure about Josiah's love too. Josiah was cheating on Abigail, but it was out of love, not just passion. This reminds me of that. Josiah kept saying he loved her. No matter what antics or magic that crazy witch cast, no matter what, he kept telling her he loved her. Just like Bryce. Through struggle and hesitation, Josiah actually loved Escoba. It makes their affair not so evil, doesn't it? Or, perhaps, just more tragic?

"I love you, Cadence," Bryce says quietly by my ear. The rain pelts the ground hard again, so hard that I almost can't hear him. "I just worry so much about you. You mean everything to me. I would give up everything I have but you. And now I want to protect you and our baby girl."

"Chandra," I say with a nod.

We don't talk anymore. But he holds me so tightly on top of him as the rain pours down outside. He squeezes me as if he never wants to let me go. And I feel that pressure again down below, as he's squeezing me so hard.

"Show me," I whisper. "Fuck me."

And he does. He runs his hands along the crack of my ass, while moving them up my body ever so gently. He's slow. And I'm just clutching him in a tight embrace, almost as if I'm worried that if I let go, he'll leave. We're so gentle. It's the opposite of what I was before. No more biting. We're both just slowly moving and touching each other. And that feels better. Maybe we were worried about hurting each other?

I sit up a little and we explore each other's chests with our hands—his hard chest and muscular abs under me. I haven't been working out lately, but Bryce has. I can feel those ripples in his torso and stomach. I run my fingers along his thin hairs, now wet from my skin, while he runs his fingers over my boobs and nipples and down to my back and the curves of my ass again. And we just move so slowly, massaging each other. Loving one another. And it's nicer.

"Shouldn't we close the door?" he asks.

"I'd rather not. It's like sex in the woods. You know how much I love that. I'm a witch. Unless you want it closed, Bryce?"

"No."

I feel his hands squeeze my butt a little hard. Then he

presses along my back and pulls me close to him again. He touches his soft lips to mine gently. My tongue enters and plays with his. And then my hands run along his short, feathery hair. My whole body lies gently over him as he massages me everywhere.

"Cadence?"

"What? Huh? Yeah?" I look down. His eyes are closed. I kiss him gently on the lips. Then I whisper, "Yeah, lover?"

"Just keep me in the loop," he says, opening his eyes. He stares into mine. "Don't keep secrets."

"I hate secrets. I've hated the secrets in Hawthorne more than anything else in the world."

I feel his cock press so deep inside. And that does it.

"Ohhh, Bryce. Shit...this is it. Slow but sure, right? Okay...I think I'm...still going to cum. I'm going to cum on you now anyway, whether passionate or gentle, because... I do love you. I do. I love you so fucking much. That's all that matters." But then I get quiet. And I just hear the sound of the pouring rain outside. And his quiet moaning. "Are you feeling good? I mean...does this...is this making you feel good?"

"Yes."

"Fuck me then," I say, clutching him tightly again. I run my lips and cheeks against the stubble of his cheek. "Yes? Oh, fuck me."

My pelvis moves up and down, pressing his cock a little harder. But still slow. Now, I lean all my weight on him, but still move slowly.

I whisper in his ear. "Love me. Love your wife."

I hear him breathe heavily and finally climax under me.

"And... Fuck, don't even...fuck, this is it, don't you try to stop me next time, Bryce! Don't you dare stop me ever again! You feel too good."

He laughs as I fall to his side.

The rain crashes outside again, as if buckets are opening up by our house. And then wind picks up, blowing cold air against our bodies. I do everything I can not to shiver. I don't want to get up from his embrace. It's such a crazy storm now. Maybe it's gonna turn into a hurricane? God, and I was alone out there pregnant! But now I'm in my hubby's arms under shelter. That's so nice.

"We've gotta get away from the rain, Kate," he says. "Let me shut the door and let me help you upstairs to shower."

"No." I shake my head. "Not yet. Just hold me. Just be with me and hold me in this storm. Whatever lies outside, we can hold each other and keep each other warm. Chandra and I are warm now in your arms."

11

DRACULA

"Let's talk about vampires," Bryce says atop our lecture stage. He's in this gorgeous sepia suit I got for him in Atlanta.

A large cartoon showing people being impaled flashes on the screen behind him. There are a few chuckles. At this point, it wouldn't be one of our lectures, you know, without some grisly photos.

I'm not on stage. I'm standing at the side of the lecture hall near the right aisle. My best friend, Madison, is standing beside me. That's a mistake. I have to keep shushing her. First of all, my BFF has never been one to keep her mouth shut in class. It's gotten us into plenty of trouble in the past, and even Alondra shut us up a few times. Second, she's totally freaked out about my wandering and won't stop talking about it.

"We believe the word *nosferatu* comes from the Romanian word *nesuferit*, which means insufferable," Bryce continues, "but nobody knows for sure." A black and white picture of a creepy emaciated guy with very long fingers and fangs takes the place of the bodies skewered on poles. "Of course, the silent film *Nosferatu* popularized this other name for the famous vampire Dracula."

"Mira thinks it was Enora that threw you into that wandering," Maddie says in a hushed voice. "She thinks it was Enora again."

I shrug. Then I yawn. Bryce and I haven't been getting a lot of sleep lately, you know. It's not just my Billington House haunting—we're so scared Enora's gonna mess with our dreams. None of my sisters are sleeping. Even Maddie has bags under her eyes. Bryce drank a few cups of coffee for the lecture this morning, but I can see his exhaustion in his eyes on stage. Poor thing.

"Mira also said," Maddie says in a hushed voice, "she wants to talk to the council about initiating you to their special order because, you know, she heard you and Bryce consulted your grimoire and poured chalk and salt around the house, casting impromptu spells to shield yourself. She said they hesitated about inviting you before, because you don't really study our arts, you're so bent on classes, but now—"

"Quiet, Maddie. We never cast any spells. And who cares about Mira's witch council?"

"I mean, we all know you're a witch, Katie," Maddie says quietly. "But Mira thinks you're starting to study the arts more seriously now. She totally loves it."

I just nod because if I say more, she'll never stop talking.

"Can you pour some chalk around Mom's house too and cast some incantations to protect my mom, your brother, and me, babe?"

I roll my eyes. The funniest—or maybe the scariest—thing is she's actually serious.

"I highly recommend you check out the original Hollywood movie," Bryce continues. "It's one of my favorites. Anyway, the context of the names is important. They tie the story in with history." A painting of a guy with long dark hair, a beard, an orange robe, a turban, and large, penetrating eyes pops up on the screen. "Dracula comes from the family name Dracul, which means 'son of the dragon.' That's the Latin translation. But the Romanian translation is more sinister, meaning 'son of the devil.'

"Vlad the Impaler did not rule Transylvania or even live in the impressive gothic cliffside Bran Castle, falsely claimed to be his home. He was only born in Transylvania. You know, there's a great deal of embellishment of the myth of Bram Stoker's *Dracula*. Of course, all the fame is thanks to Bram Stoker's wonderful novel—another thing I highly recommend to you guys. Bram Stoker chose to feature Vlad as a vampire because of his infamy." He pauses and looks down at his remote slide controller. Then he presses a button. "Vlad the Impaler's favorite type of torture was, of course, to impale victims. A wood or metal pole was stuck through the anus or vagina—"

A diagram of methods of impaling a body shows up on the screen. There are moans. But some laughter. Then another groan. The groan comes from me. This image is a bit too much, Bryce.

"They tried to avoid vital organs so that the sufferer could be in agony as long as possible while being displayed to every passerby."

As I gaze around the lecture hall, nobody's talking. Yep, this is good ole shock treatment, made famous by Dr. Alondra Johansen. The only one not staring at the stage is Kenosha.

Kenosha's wearing her curly wig and a darker suit than Bryce's and mine, rummaging through papers at her desk in the front row. As much as Kenosha can drive me crazy, you gotta hand it to her. She could probably stay calm and collected even if actual impaled bodies were brought onstage.

"How is it even safe to do the rehearsal now, Kates?" Maddie asks me, "if Enora entered your dreams and made you wander?"

"Shush. She didn't."

"She didn't. Then who did?"

"What rehearsal, Maddie? Just be quiet, won't you?"

"The practice."

"Huh? Maddie, what? We can still have our Sabbath."

I turn and Maddie looks pissed.

"*Our parents*, Katie." She's lifting her eyebrows and looking at me like I'm a complete moron. "Remember? How are we going to rehearse *the wedding* next week?"

"Maybe they should just not do it," I say with a smirk.

"Vlad the Impaler lived from 1431 to 1476 in Wallachia, not Transylvania," Bryce says. "He was imprisoned during a large part of his life. Such was the strife in the region. Wallachia, and nearby Transylvania, was a land in constant conflict between crusaders and the Ottoman Empire. We should put this all in context. His reputation as the most vicious and most monstrous ruler in Europe happened while ruling in a literal living hell."

"I should slug you," Maddie whispers.

I turn and, though it sounds funny, she looks really pissed.

"Sorry, Maddie. I don't know. But, maybe, until we do Mira's service, we should delay the rehearsal? I don't know if it's safe."

"Well, we've set a date, Katie. Is that why Kenosha's here now?" she points to Kenosha in the front row. "To make sure Enora doesn't do anything funny in class?"

"She's here because she's our history dean. She just wants to make sure the class stays first rate."

"No, Cadence," Maddie says quietly, shaking her head. "No. You told me she rarely shows up. She's here to protect you and Bryce."

"Maddie, fine," I snap in a hushed whisper. "Whatever. Just shush. I don't know, okay. We have to just...carry on. Right?" A few kids in the aisles are turning to us. I got worked up and was too loud. "All we can do is live," I whisper. "If Enora wants to come here and fight me, that's her thing. Let her come out in the open and do it. I haven't once purposefully attacked her. That's all I know."

"I know," she whispers, touching my arm. "I know, Kates. That's why we're all going to try Mira's séance. We can ask Alondra if she's haunting you and pestering Enora, right? But, if you remember, Mira's planned the meeting with the coven *after* the wedding rehearsal. So, what I'm saying is...should we even have the rehearsal next week, High Priestess?"

"No, I think we should never have it."

And finally she slaps my shoulder. I mean, *really* hard.

A large map including Hungary and the Ottoman Empire shines behind the stage as Bryce walks, deep in thought.

"So there's this story that Vlad impaled two priests to get them to heaven faster," Bryce says. The audience laughs. "Or another one where dignitaries wearing turbans met with him and he decided to nail their hats to their heads. Vlad supposedly executed thousands of people with the horrible torture technique that penned his name. The one I showed you. He was a devil for sure. Many believe he was inflicted with madness, like the past Roman emperors Caligula and Nero. And yet, as I said before, we must understand that this is a man who lived in, possibly, the most dangerous region of Europe at the time. He fought the Transylvanian Saxons of the north, later ethnic Germans, and the Ottoman Empire of the South, later Turkey. He was stuck right dab in the center of perpetual war. So, this setting created the most ruthless ruler ever known. But not only was Vlad Dracul infamous, press amplified his infamy for readers all over Europe, particularly Germany and Russia, with the invention of the movable printing press, which happened during his reign, in the 1450s. In fact, these stories are among the first known popular readings of the time because of this new printing invention.

"So...you all tell me—was Vlad the Impaler a devil, simply a product of his place and time? Or was he a nosferatu? An actual vampire? Personally, I think he was a devil." He gestures with an outstretched arm to the map behind him. "One of the most evil people in the world."

Then Bryce presses his remote again.

The slide changes to a portrait. Only...it's not Vlad the Impaler. There's an explosion of gasps. Because the slide is a headshot of my own personal devil, Dr. Alondra Johansen.

"What in the hell?" shouts a student.

Shock changes to mirth as the hall bursts into laughter.

Kenosha finally raises her eyes from her papers. Then she jumps up from her seat and turns to me. Bryce furrows his brow and presses a button on his handheld controller over and over, but he can't change the slide.

He rushes back to the podium.

The screen shuts off.

"Okay...that's it," Bryce says, sounding uneasy. "Well, guess we're graced with another picture of my predecessor—" He chuckles nervously. "No...not the most evil person in the world. Anyway, read about the Ottoman Empire. The printing press. The crusades. There's a lot more here than just the legend of a vampire. There's going to be a quiz about all this stuff on Thursday."

12

BY ACCIDENT

I'M SITTING WITH MADDIE AND JOSIE, IN THE MIDDLE ROW, under the vaulted ceiling in Hawthorne Church. It's nice. The drapes are open on the window by our bench, letting in the clear morning sunlight. And right now, the priest is preaching about love.

"We know and believe in the love that God has for us," says the priest. The priest is an older man, balding, with gray hair and glasses. He is wearing an umber suit. "God is love." He pauses and nods, as if savoring those words. "God is love." I'm remembering Frida bowing her head and whispering stuff like this during sermons. Frida's whole life is devoted to God, and that's one of the reasons I loved going with her so much. She's the one who got me to go every week, after all. I miss her so much. "And he that dwelleth in love, dwelleth in God, and God in him."

Josie is a believer too. She's been Christian since before Alondra recruited her. Of course, Maddie was raised by a green witch, Aunt Jane, and has been more like an atheist, like me. My BFF is just here because I asked her to accompany me. Speaking of love, Maddie loves me.

"This is John 4:16," continues the pastor. "It is saying that God is not only about love, he *is* love. This is so significant. Think of what this means if you don't take God into your life. We are not perfect. God is perfect. But the most important thing is that God forgives all of our sins."

And he pauses for everybody to think about that. Then, before more words come out of his mouth—

Bang!

I hear an explosive crash. It sounds like something smashed into the wall of the church. Then it's followed by another crash. And another. And then a horn honking.

There's some shouting and a disturbance that I think is coming from the parking lot. A few people at the back of the church rush out the door behind us. Josie, who's closest to the small window by the bench, rushes to it. But she shakes her head, apparently not seeing anything.

Bang!

There's another crash.

"It's a car accident in the parking lot," cries someone at the back of the church.

There's another bang. Nearly everyone's standing up at this point. The pastor is leaning on a podium squinting and peering down the aisle. People are rushing to the door.

And a car horn keeps blaring.

Bang! Bang!

There it is again. It's weird. If it's an accident, why does it keep happening? Again and again? All of us quickly head to the exit.

"Single file, please," hollers the pastor. "Safely. Be careful, there's no reason to rush."

But the church is really crowded. School just started so there are a lot of newbies coming to Sunday services, and I have to wait in line just to exit. When I finally get outside, I see a huge crowd surrounding a car. *My car!* I had parked my car backward in the parking lot for an easy exit. Butting up against the hood is a dilapidated white pickup truck. The front hood of my car is smoking. The metal of the white truck is crunched and folded against my hood. And leaning against the pickup, with arms folded, is Enora. She's wearing her usual black dress with a collar. And she's just standing there watching us rush over amid the incessant honking from my car alarm.

"What's going on!" I cry. "Shit! What the hell did you do to my car, Enora!"

"You fucking bitch," Maddie shouts. "What did you do to Katie's car!"

Maddie walks right up to Enora's face ready to hit her. Enora doesn't flinch. She just glares at Maddie. Then, despite my best friend's bravado, Maddie steps back. I think Maddie remembers the terror this bitch-witch caused her when Maddie joined her Abaddon coven.

"I'm doing the same shit Windstorm's doing to my coven, Blackbird," Enora says, snarling. "I'm fighting back in the only way she understands. She'll never understand spells and witchcraft. I thought maybe she'd understand this."

I look around and there are like fifty people surrounding us now. This is not a good time to cast the spell I want to cast. I'm tempted to hurl her against a tree trunk, or impale her with a tree branch, as she suggested in Meadow Park during the black magic spell we performed together.

"What the hell's wrong with you?" I shout. "Huh? You want my attention, Enora? Fine! You got it. Now why the hell are you trashing my car?"

"Your car, Katie?" Then she smirks. "I thought this was Alondra's?"

And that honking just makes it worse. Over and over I keep hearing the blaring of my horn. My heart's racing. My fists are tight. I watch as a shadow is cast over Enora. The parking lot quickly darkens under passing clouds—caused by my magic.

Enora just smirks.

"Nuh-uh-uh, Katie," Enora says, "you might want to be careful what you cast around these zealot friends of yours."

"I prefer Christians over Thelemites!"

"I never said I was a Thelemite. I'm an Enora-nite. I worship myself." And the bitch flashes her left hand—the hand with the pentagram tattoo.

"*I don't care what the hell you are! Why'd you just crash into my car, you fucking cunt!*"

"God, watch your language, Cadence," Enora says, feigning shock. "Tsk, tsk, aren't we on church grounds? Why, this is a church parking lot. Where are your manners? Does your god want you to be cursing like that? Where's Bryce, by the way? Isn't he a nice Christian like you? I'm sure you plan to make your whole nice family Christian, right? You all planning to come here every Sunday holding hands? With your unborn daughter, Chandra?"

"*Are you threatening her now!*"

"You attack me, I attack you," Enora says, raising her brow.

"I think I'm going to kill her, Maddie," I say, cocking my head back. "Maybe I should use her own deranged magic against her on my grounds."

"No, Cadence," Maddie says. "No."

Maddie looks around nervously at all the crowds. There are so many people. A few have their cellphones out recording Enora's show as we're yelling at each other.

"Fine, you got my attention!" I exclaim. "Now what the hell do you want?"

"What's the meaning of this?" shouts the pastor, rushing up to us.

"Just a car accident, Father," Enora says. Then she makes me sick when she winks at him and gives him a disgusting, lascivious smile.

"Seems deliberate," the pastor says, shaking his head.

"Up until now, Katie," Enora says, turning her back to the priest, "I've accepted your fucking virgin ineptitude. See, I think you're so ignorant that you don't understand what the hell's going on in Hawthorne. In the past, I've used your occult ignorance and innocence for my benefit. But now, in order to protect my coven, seems I'm going to have to teach you a lesson."

"I'm calling the police," the pastor says, rushing off.

"You invoked Alondra on Hilltop Bluff to save Bryce a few years ago," Enora continues. She has to speak loudly. The horn is still blaring. "Do you remember? I remember. Then her ghost nearly threw me off the cliff after you *evoked* her, summoning her into this world. You didn't save me, you conjured her spirit to attack me. But you did save me in Alabama. I haven't forgotten that. That is the only reason you're still alive. But the nightmares my sisters are suffering have to stop. I warned you when you were with your coven, but you haven't heeded my warning. It's still happening. Worst of all, I don't think you even know how to stop it. I could help—"

"I'm not casting spells on you! Why do you keep accusing me?"

"Am I accusing poor little Katie?" she derides, pretending to cry.

"I just might start casting something now!"

"Cadence," Maddie warns, "shh, everyone's watching."

She's right.

"The magic isn't coming from Melanie," Enora says. "It's not Samhain, and Aamon's dead. So who's casting, dummy? Someone who should never have been a witch. You hardly even know how to cast a spell because all you do is study. *You study the wrong fucking things!* Our arts are not school. That was a ruse by our teacher so she could be accepted and practice in silence." Enora looks around at the crowd. Her stupid smile only widens. "And now you come here to be preached to about *love?*"

Enora lifts her hand and snaps her fingers. The honking from my car stops. I doubt the onlookers realize they just witnessed magic.

"A real witch only distinguishes good and dark energies, Cadence," she snaps. Despite my horn having stopped, the bitch isn't talking any more quietly. "Your insistence on questioning good versus evil as a Christian insults real witches. I've told you time and time again that I'm about *me*. I believe in Satanic *me*. And it's religious institutions like this one that will never understand *me*. It fucking insults *me*!"

"What the hell do your beliefs or magic spells have to do with you driving into my fucking car, Enora!"

"This isn't your car, it's Alondra's car, isn't it?" Enora asks, raising a finger to my face. I bat her hand down. "It's got a lot to do with you, *Allie*. Just like this church, you will never understand me. You're not a real witch. Alondra should never have made you her successor. She should have passed her wand over to me. This car should have been mine!"

"Windstorm is my successor and High Priestess," I say. "I've cast you out." But that wasn't my voice. That was Alondra's.

I hear gasps. People around me step back. Not Enora. Enora doesn't look afraid—she seems more pissed than ever.

"Who abandoned who, teacher!" Enora shouts in my face. *"All I ever did was hear your incessant bitching about losing everyone you cared about! Never me! You cast me out for practicing the same magic you taught your own husband!"*

"*Vade retro*, Enora," Alondra's voice says calmly. "*Vade retro*. Get out of Hawthorne. I cast you out of this town. Never step foot here again and leave Cadence alone."

"Not yet," Enora says smugly. Then she wags her finger at me. "Not yet. *You* get out of Hawthorne, Cadence. Had Alondra chosen the right disciple, all this misdirected necromancy would never have manifested."

Sirens blare. We hear the police cars before we see them.

Then they make it up the hill and surround the church parking lot.

"Enough shit," Enora says with a smirk. "I didn't total your car only for you, dear Amica. I hated Alondra too. Don't worry. Next time we meet, Cadence, I won't fight in your language, I'll fight you in mine. No more warnings. The next time I come, it will cripple you, you crying, whiny bitch!"

Then her body bursts into a flock of crows. There are echoing caws. All the people surrounding us gasp. So many black birds rush from her body that some of their wings collide with me.

"*Descendere!*" I shout, staring up at the sky. There are so many birds that they've blocked the sun. "*Descendere!*" A few birds fall to the ground, but many more rush off into the trees surrounding the parking lot.

"Which bird, Windstorm?" Enora's voice asks, laughing. "Go cower in your church and hate everyone who doesn't worship God. *You* get out of this town! You and your teacher! Get the fuck out before you destroy my circle in Atlanta and Hawthorne *BY ACCIDENT!*"

A few birds shake on the ground around the parked cars. My spell caused them to fall. One is shaking on the remaining pieces of Enora's ripped black dress. But the bitch is right, none of them transforms into her.

Maddie and Josie aren't searching the sky; they're staring at the smoke coming from the hood of my wrecked car. Enora's jalopy probably looks the same as it did before the accident. It's a totaled wreck she probably stole just to crash into mine.

"I'm sorry, Cadence," Josie says, staring.

"What's happening here?" asks a short policewoman, rushing up to us. Her hair is in a bun.

"Everyone, go back to business," says an officer by her side. "Whoever's cars are here, stay. Otherwise, please leave the area."

The crowds die down. Then I realize with horror that all these witnesses from church saw Enora's transformation.

Not only is my hood crumbled in half, but Enora's violence managed to cave in the steering wheel and front dashboard. The windshield is shattered and bent. And one of the front tires is sideways. There's nothing left of the car. Alondra's bougie car is totaled.

"Whose car is this?" asks the lady officer.

"Mine," I mutter, staring at the smoke.

"Were you inside when it was damaged?"

I shake my head.

"Cadence," says the pastor, running over. "Where's that woman that did this?"

"She flew away."

13

NO ONE IS GOOD

I'm sitting on a couch beside Bryce sipping from a huge steamy mug of tea. The tea was Aunt Jane's idea. I didn't ask for anything. She sort of just handed me the drink when Maddie and I came through the door of her house. The tea is soothing. And the steam keeps forming a nice fog moistening my forehead and cheeks. I have no idea what's in the tea, but it's wonderful. It's probably some spell from Aunt Jane's green witchcraft.

But my heart's racing. I'm wishing that I could make Enora materialize here right now so I could slug her across the face.

Occasionally Bryce leans closer, and I lean my head on his shoulder. *Sigh*... But then, there's Dad. With all the stress going on right now, hearing my dad talking in the kitchen with Aunt Jane is unnerving.

Maddie's standing by the sliding door, staring out at their garden. The last time she looked like this I had killed that sweet woman, Agnes. Mira's on a couch across from us, sitting with Courtney, staring at her cellphone. Courtney's leaning her head on Mira's shoulder. So we're all together at Aunt Jane's again. It's like our meeting place when everything turns to shit.

I'm so pissed. Like, I am so absolutely, *totally pissed off! Like, what absolutely positively the fuck is wrong with that piece-of-shit bitch!*

Before I open my mouth to vent more to my friends, I'm surprised by a small girl running down the hallway to the kitchen. I hear my dad and Aunt Jane laugh and offer her a cookie. A second later, she rushes by us in the living room, nearly hitting her head on the sliding glass door. I think if it weren't for her reflection, she would have run right through the glass.

"Careful, Sophie!" cries a woman. I recognize that voice, but I just can't place it. It sounds like someone from...*Brooklyn?*

"Oh, hello, Cadence," says Pamela, grabbing little Sophie's hand. "Maddie."

Maddie pushes away from the glass door to greet Liam's wife, Pamela. She embraces the older woman. Pamela's about Aunt Jane's age, with long blond hair.

She's wearing slacks and a dark blouse. And following Pamela is, of course, the man himself. (Remember, the man who I recently went nuts over after hearing that he brought that devil Bill Reardon to Hawthorne to have ceremonial sex with all my friends? Yeah, that Liam).

Liam's wearing his ratty Yankee baseball cap and jeans. He's all smiley. Why is he in such a good mood?

I look down at the steam from my mug. Then I stop staring at it because it reminds me of the steam coming from the hood of Alondra's car.

"Hi, Cadence," Liam says with a nod. "It's good to see you."

Maddie takes him into her arms. "Hi, Liam."

"You guys didn't tell me you were coming to town," I say, pulling away from Bryce. "Bryce, this is Liam's wife, Pam, and that's their daughter Sophia. You know Liam."

"The girl who nearly ran through the glass door?" asks Bryce.

"I know, she's a bit clumsy," Pamela says with a laugh.

"She's cute," Bryce says.

He gets up and shakes Pamela's hand. Then he looks real cute when he kneels down and shakes little Sophie's hand too.

"Hi," Sophie says.

"We brought the whole clan this time," Liam says to me with a grin.

"Great," I comment.

"Another witch bothering you?" Liam asks me, putting his hands in his pockets. He loses his smile after I feel a scowl form on my face.

"She just fucking wrecked your car," I say with a shrug.

"My car?" Liam asks, furrowing his brow.

"She drove into our car at church," Bryce explains. "Alondra's old Jaguar. She totaled it. Then she threatened to curse our coven again. Enora's only getting worse."

"That's not very magical," Liam says.

"She turned herself into—" I am about to say "birds" when Dad walks into the room with Aunt Jane. And, gross, he's holding Jane's hand. I am so weirded out by Dad knowing about our magic. Even though he knows we cast real magic, I don't want to talk about it in front of him.

But then Mira, who's shaking Liam's hand now, says, "She transformed herself into a flock of ravens. This is my girlfriend, Courtney."

I quickly look at Pam. She doesn't seem the least bit bothered about a woman being turned into black birds. I wonder if she's seen Liam cast magic before? And their daughter sure doesn't care. Sophie's busying herself on the carpet with a puzzle that Maddie just brought over.

"They're really worried, Lee," Dad says to Liam. He offers Liam a firm handshake. Liam introduces his wife and points at their daughter. "They don't know why she's angry at Cadence,"

Dad says, "but she claims they're attacking her. I'm so glad you're here for Katie and Bryce."

This is *so* cringy. It actually upsets me more.

I gaze through the glass at Jane's lovely yard. It's seems to be beckoning me away from everyone. I think I prefer flowers over people at the moment. (Not you. You can keep snooping, I suppose. Just bear in mind that I am in a really foul mood.)

"Well, we came here to watch my favorite lady get married, Rick," Liam says, smiling at Jane.

Why is he so fucking jolly? I mean, why is anybody happy about my life being turned upside down at the moment? Dad's getting married to Aunt Jane? Wonderful.

I walk outside alone.

It's cloudy and a little cold. It looks like it might rain judging from the gray clouds forming, but it's so pretty with all of Aunt Jane's perfectly manicured plants and flowers. It smells of jasmine and roses. That's nice. Even the grass is perfectly manicured.

I've seen how Jane cuts her grass. She cuts it with scissors. No, I'm not kidding. She really spends all her time outside and, when she cuts her grass, she crouches on her knees and cuts each blade. I used to think it was weird when Maddie and I'd come for dinner, or I was staying over, and she'd be outside in her small yard for hours at a time. She absolutely loves being outside. I think she likes it even more than people. Because, you know, people can be tiresome.

I sit down on a wooden chair.

Then I look at the perfectly cut grass under my flat black boots.

The door slides open. Of all people, can you guess who it is? Liam.

He pulls over another wooden chair. Jane has about five of them, some folded, in her small yard.

"Mind some company?" he asks.

Kind of.

I look at him and he lurches back.

"Your eyes, Cadence. They're not yours. They're green."

I cover my eyes.

"We're going to attempt a séance to get rid of her. You suggested I scry. I scried. It did nothing. Now everyone's suspecting Alondra is attacking Enora through me. That's why Enora attacked me."

"No, you'd know if Alondra was casting through you."

I shake my head. "You sound so sure. Enora thinks the opposite."

"I think you're too powerful a witch to not know when someone is casting spells through you," he says, "whether it be a ghost—or even my wife. No, I don't believe that, Cadence."

"I didn't know when Enora was cursing me a few years ago. Or even a few months ago, when her voodoo oungan was cursing me. I'm not that powerful, Liam. I don't know what's going on half the time in Hawthorne."

"Because you don't believe in yourself," he says, pressing my shoulder with his finger. And he has this stupid smile again, acting so fucking holly jolly.

"Well, we're gonna run a séance. My friend Mira knows séances better than any of us. And if that doesn't work, we'll try good ole useless shield spells with Kenosha again."

"Why don't you tell me more about this witch? This Enora?"

"How about you tell me something, Mr. Johansen," I ask, facing him. And I'm too pissed to care if my eyes are green or not.

Control yourself. Don't take this too far, Cadence.

But, I mean, look at him—he's got this huge grin on his face. Is it funny that my car's wrecked? Or that his former wicked witch wife is possessing me? Why would anyone be happy at the moment?

Are you having a nice day? In a good mood? Well, good for you. A witch just fucking crashed into my car, okay?

Liam nods at me slowly and stupidly. Then I look down, thinking of how the hell I'm going to ask my next question.

"I was in the library a couple weeks ago," I say. "Alondra was teaching me in our book, *Broomstick*, about Eliphas Levi for my upcoming thesis. But then she started talking about gender. And then she spoke of sacrifice. She spoke about dark magic, Mr. Johansen, involving students, girls, and virgins. Then she mentioned you. Know what I'm talking about?"

He doesn't answer. He just furrows his brow. But I'm quite sure he knows exactly what I'm talking about.

"She mentioned you. So...did you? Were you involved in the same sex ceremonies as your *friend,* Professor Reardon? The same sex magick?"

He doesn't answer. He turns from me looking like he's ready to stand up and go. Yep, not so jolly anymore.

"I hated Reardon. He raped my best friend, Maddie. Did you know that? You know, Jane's daughter. But, according to Alondra, Reardon was your best friend. Is that true, Mr. Johansen? Was Professor Reardon, that sick fuck, your best friend?"

"Yes."

"Were you involved in those same rituals with innocent students?"

"You don't need to know that," he says, looking back into my eyes. Now he's pissed. I don't think he cares whether my eyes are brown or green. "I know everything you're going through is tearing you apart, but what you're asking now is my business, not yours, Cadence."

"Were you a part of those sex ceremonies or not? Bryce was, but he claims he only...did it with Enora. Did you take innocent students and perform *ceremonies,* Liam? Why is it that everyone who's supposed to mentor me, teach me, lies and covers everything up in secrets. Why can't you all just tell me the truth? Were you? And how is it not my business? Alondra's coven is now my coven. Alondra's *sex magick* coven."

Yeah, well...he gets up.

"Was Jane involved in sex magick too?"

"Of course not! Not Jane."

"Okay," I coax. "What about you?"

"When Winona died, Cadence, it was enough for me," he says, running his hand over his thin hair. "After killing a little girl, I had had it with our magic. But before...yes, I did horrible things. I already told you I did horrible things."

"What sort of things?"

He's done. He's not here to comfort me anymore; he wants to get the hell away from me. Why? Because he fucked virgin students with my former teacher.

"You moved Allie and your coven away from all that," he says, shaking his head. "Bill was a good friend of mine, yes, but dark magic destroyed him. He wasn't the man I knew when we were friends. He changed for me and for Alondra. It's terrible what happened to him. You didn't know the Bill I knew. He was a good man, Cadence, I tell you, before he dabbled in Allie's witchcraft. The black magic transformed him. He was a good man."

"*Bill Reardon was never a good man! He was a horrible man.* My friends trusted him. When I first joined the circle, he hid his perversions in front of us, using mandrake to make us susceptible. He and your former wife pretended it was to study ritual and magic. Then he used drugs to ceremonially rape my friend! Your friend's daughter!"

Liam walks to the sliding door.

"You have no right to hide things from me!"

"I've never hidden anything from you, Cadence," he says. "You came to me. Look, I'm sorry for what happened to your car."

"I don't care about my fucking car! It was Alondra's car! Liam, if Bryce hadn't protected me, your friend would have done the same thing to me on my initiation. And if my dearest, sweetest friend Frida hadn't joined late, god...I can't even imagine! He would have ruined her too! Why'd you bring William Reardon to Hawthorne? How could you do that!"

"I didn't bring him! Alondra did! You're upset with what my friend did sexually to your friends? Alondra did those same things to students, Cadence! Why damn Bill and me, but not your former teacher?"

The room spins. I feel sick. My eyes close and I feel a sinking feeling.

My eyes open to that horrible man helping me sit back down in the chair. I look down and the green grass and white lily petals spin under me. I'm feeling nauseous, like I want to throw up again. Is it my pregnancy? Or am I just that mad?

Clouds shade the backyard now. And there's a smell. It's not pleasant like flowers—it's rank like blood and excrement. The sun is shrouded in darkness. Is this my magic, or Liam's? It feels so dark, so cold—like dark magic.

Liam has his hand on me, but his hand feels icy cold. And it is shaking. Then, as I gaze up into his eyes, he's not looking like he wants to comfort me. He looks like he wants to kill me.

"I'm not your teacher!" he snaps in a broken voice, kneeling beside me. "I never said I was. You came to me, and I didn't want to help you. Remember? Did you ever think about why? I wanted nothing to do with this town. Only when I saw you were in trouble did I come. But I'm not here for you. This isn't about you. I'm here for my friend who's getting married to your father, Cadence."

Is that supposed to make me feel better? But he hardly waits for a response. He turns his back on me and storms back into the house.

I don't care. I just crouch over in the chair with my head in my hands. I hear Liam shout something at Aunt Jane. It's something about how I'm impossible. That reminds me of Alondra. If she were alive, that's exactly what she'd be saying about me now. Why? Because I'm bringing out into the open something totally disgusting that neither of them should have done. Something they're hiding from everybody. Something that shouldn't be *occult*.

"What's the matter, Lee?" Pamela asks.

God, does Pamela not know about his sins?!

I don't know if he left the living room or just stopped talking, but, despite all the guests in the house, it gets quiet outside. I like the fact that I can't hear him now.

My eyes tear up. But I don't cry. You know, the woman who drove into my car today hardened me against doing that.

The sliding door opens again. Maddie says something. I don't look up. Then I feel someone come from behind, kneel by my side, and embrace me.

"Maddie?" I ask. "Maddie, he did it."

"Katie, are you feeling sick again?" Bryce asks quietly, rubbing my back. "Liam said you were sick? Is it the pregnancy, babe?"

"He did it, Bryce," I say quietly, shaking my head.

"Who?" Bryce asks. "Who did what?"

"Liam practiced sex magick. With... Alondra."

Goety, goety, goety.

"I know he did, Cadence."

14

BUILDING INSPECTORS

I HAVE A VERY STRANGE, UNSETTLING FEELING AS BRYCE AND I make our way up the hill toward the Billington House. Even walking up this hill, on this dirt path, under this dense forest is creepy. I remember being freaked out the first time I came with Maddie, the night of my first kiss with my hubby. Well, just as I held hands with my bestie then, I have Bryce's hand firmly in mine now. I know I'm a badass witch and all, but that doesn't mean I don't get scared. And between the hooting of owls and the rustle in the bushes on this dark cold night...it's...well, it's creepy.

We're wearing snow coats. It's getting that cold, far colder than normal in early October. That's bad because, honestly, who knows how long we'll be inside the house for our séance tomorrow, and I seriously doubt they have any indoor heating working yet.

When we pass a few more trees, I spot the house up at the top of the hill. Only the first floor is complete, and even that has boarded-up windows, ladders, paint cans, and metal and wood scaffolding. In a few sections, the second floor has been started, with walls rising, and there's even scaffolding going up higher in some parts, but mostly the structure is only one floor high. The Billington House was a three-story structure before it was burned to the ground. Bryce tells me they're planning on rebuilding it exactly like it was before.

I can just make out a central window—you know, the one I freakishly stood naked in front of holding a candle and acting like Abigail's ghost in my wandering. Well, there's glass there now, but the window is full of tape. The front door is boarded up. And there's half a ton of "no trespassing" signs surrounding the front façade on a dirt lot.

"Katie, you're shaking," Bryce says, rubbing my hands. "I should have gotten you gloves to keep warm."

"Who said I'm cold. The Billington House is scary."

"Well, we gotta keep Chandra warm," he says, rubbing my belly.

Ah, I squeeze him tightly over that.

"You sure you you want to be here?" he asks. "You don't have to. I can meet with him alone tonight to arrange everything with our sisters."

"Then I won't be in your arms all the way back home, babe." I sigh. "I don't know, Bryce. Why does it seem we have some sort of standoff every few months here in Hawthorne? Before I came into your life, was Hawthorne always this crazy?"

"The years under Reardon and Alondra were pretty mundane. Not much happened, except..."

I know we're close to the front of the house, because all the grass and trees have been cleared from this part of the path. It's just a large dirt lot with all the trees and bushes gone. It's dead —perfect for a party. And that's the plan. Not only are we planning on holding a séance here—the fraternity wants to throw their Halloween party here in a few weeks, if the city will allow it.

"Except what?"

"Except Enora," Bryce answers. "And except the rituals you

don't want me to discuss. But most of the drama was Enora. Knowing her, you can only imagine how our breakup worked out."

"It must have been terrible."

"Yeah. Alondra, of course, protected me. But I don't think Alondra ever really liked Enora and me together even when we dated. When we broke up, I needed her protection, especially at night."

"Bitch."

He nods. "And then Alondra had her falling out with Enora after the affair. Then, for a little while, Alondra faced tough times like you. Enora was actually more furious about being thrown out of the coven than breaking up with me. Her magic was a handful even for Falconsong."

"What did Alondra do different? How'd she keep it all together?"

"Nothing, Cadence." He glances at me and frowns. "You always think Alondra did everything better than you. She didn't. She had as many difficulties with our circle as you have. Maybe more. But even though the coven's struggling so much lately, I really think you're a positive force, babe. I always have."

"That's sweet, Bryce, but I think I'm struggling a lot more than she did. Maybe Liam struggled as much as I do. I always felt close to him, you know. We both had to deal so closely with Alondra. But then I went crazy when I heard what he did. I shouted at him at Maddie's house. He barely said a word. But he said Alondra did all those rites with men too."

"Everyone heard your fight inside."

"I shouldn't look up to either of them. I suppose it sounds like our wicked mentor didn't have it easy either."

"To live is to struggle," he says, squeezing my hand and shrugging.

"Well, I wouldn't call being possessed by your former

teacher and dealing with an ancient ancestor curse normal living. Sure is a struggle though."

We stop walking when we get close to the entrance.

Then I turn to him. I can just see the Billington House ruins over his left shoulder now. I press his nose with a finger. Then I reach up on my tippy toes, put my arms around him, and kiss his lips.

"I love Hawthorne, despite all our troubles."

"You love being a witch?"

"No. I love being with you here. Isn't that enough?"

He nods. And we kiss some more. I like it. He's warm.

"That you, Bryce?" cries a voice.

We turn and a man is jutting out of one of the windows. The front door is completely boarded up, but one of the windows is open.

"Yeah. Jared, Katie's pregnant and it's freezing out here. Come on, get us in quick."

"I'm fine, Bryce."

I wave at Jared, who's still halfway out the window. Jared's a short, stocky guy with feathery blond hair wearing a green checkered flannel button-down. A real nice, fun guy. One of Bryce's besties from his old fraternity—the fraternity that owns the Billington House.

"Hi Cadence," Jared says. "You guys ready to do whatever the hell weird stuff your group does? Rumor has it that the provost was arranging some of this, so it can't all be illegal. Right? Well, I don't know why you're here. But let me remind you, Bryce, neither do the police. Let's keep it that way. The house hasn't passed inspection yet."

"Never mind, man," Bryce says. "Just open the front door."

"Can't. It's boarded up."

"We have to go through the window?" Bryce asks, rolling his eyes.

"Entrée," Jared says with a wider smile, gesturing to the window.

"Sorry, Cadence, but we'll have to climb in," Bryce says. "Can you do it? There's no door."

"I'm not *that* pregnant, Bryce."

We climb through the small window.

It's warmer inside—just a little. I hug Jared. Then he gestures to the hallway. He turns on a large flashlight because it's super dark. Bryce and I switch on our cellphone lights.

Our shoes echo along the cement flooring. We pass that famous window—you know the window I was weirdly standing in front of in the form of Abigail—the huge window Abigail's ghost is said to haunt. I really hate seeing it. Then we pass by what once was the kitchen, but now there are only a few wooden cabinets. Looking back, I see a very large shadowed entryway and a hallway. In darkness, a lot of the hallways look the same.

"Spooky, eh?" Jared asks with a laugh. "Ain't it fun?"

"The fraternity is making the building exactly like it was?" I ask him. My voice echoes in darkness.

"No, we aren't doing anything, Cadence," he says. "The state of Georgia is. This was deemed a historic site. Fortunately for us, all we need to do is preserve the outside façade. They don't care what we do inside. Which, as your husband will attest to, can get pretty crazy. Especially good ole Bryce Wallace and his past exploits."

I lightly slap Bryce's back. "What's he mean by that?"

"Jared is exaggerating," Bryce says.

"That's what you always say, Bryce."

"'Cause it's true," Bryce says with a shrug. "I was pretty boring."

"I wouldn't say boring," says Jared. "You certainly drank like a fish."

"*Drank*, Cadence," Bryce says, turning to me. "That's all. *Drank*."

"What else was he talking about?"

I laugh. I can barely see Bryce's face. I know him well enough by now to "see" his expression in my mind though.

"Here's the room," Jared says, gesturing with a broad sweep of his hand.

I don't see much, until Jared flashes his large flashlight around. I remember this room so well. I ran out after Mira's séance last time. This is the living room. I really don't have to look. I can almost picture it vividly in my mind.

I recall the large dining room table, with a red tablecloth, at the center. And in the center there was a large crystal ball surrounded by candles. A very young Mira was wearing a dark dress. It was too tight, indecently showing her bosom. She was waving her fingers over the planchette of a Ouija board. The board was a toy. And Mira was totally overdoing her theatrics. I don't think Mira knew what the hell she was doing back then. I remember black drapes over the windows. Right now, shining the light at the outer wall, I see that the windows are boarded up, giving the same dark effect. I remember everything being coated in dust. I couldn't stop sneezing. Now it doesn't affect me. All the dust and mold burned up in the fire, I suppose. This was one of the only rooms in the house that hadn't been transformed into a frat room for Psi Kappa Psi, and, because of that, I wasn't the only person who avoided it during parties over the years. It always sort of creeped everyone out too much. But now, the place is just a large empty, unfinished room with cement flooring—perfect for a séance with my coven.

"You guys said you're bringing the fold-out tables?" Bryce asks.

"They're coming," Jared says with a nod. "Give us some time, man."

"Dude, we need it this week," Bryce says. And he takes out his cellphone. "Our meeting is this Friday, Jared."

"All right, all right, don't worry. We'll get 'em. I just gotta get a team to bring them in from the backyard. Remember, we had them in a storage shed and brought them out during Beltane."

"Katie and I have a team. I just need to know where they are, and our friends can get it all set up."

"What you guys planning?" asks Jared. "Come on. You can tell me, Bryce. I can keep a secret. I was chapter president. Remember?"

"This is too hush-hushed even for a chapter president, man."

15

AUNT JANE'S MAGIC

In the wild grass glade of my backyard, my friends and family are in line, each holding a bouquet of garden roses, lilacs, and peonies. I'm wearing sunglasses to shade my eyes from the bright sun above. Some of the fall trees surrounding us are turning red, orange, and yellow, and many of the leaves have fallen. It smells fresh and clean, like my backyard always smells, but there's a nice added flowery scent emanating from my hands. And, aside from rather stifling lilac silk dresses, all of my sisters are acting giddy and having fun.

"Get on with it," says Mira, complaining. "Enough is enough, Aunt Jane."

Mira looks so weird. It honestly might be the first time I've ever seen her not wearing black. I mean, she even wore black officiating at Bryce's and my wedding. All the bridesmaids in the party are wearing lilac and, with all Mira's demon tattoos on her neck, along with her thin scar, she doesn't look good when she tries looking normal.

"Quiet, Meer," snaps Courtney, beside her. "She just wants the perfect wedding. I think it's nice."

Courtney's not even in the wedding party. Courtney's

standing in for Uncle Hanley, who isn't in town yet. But Mira's right. Aunt Jane is taking forever to arrange our line.

"Hold on, just hold on," Aunt Jane says. "Just one more check. Something's still not right. Liam, I think you should switch with Bryce."

No!

First off, we've done this walk four times already! Second, if Liam switches with Bryce, that means *I'm* going to be walking down the aisle with creepo. I'm still not talking to him. I know, maybe you think I'm being ridiculous. I mean, I forgave Alondra, or... actually, well, I never really forgave you, Alondra, but I always hated Reardon more than you. And Liam was his best friend! I can't get over that. I also liked the idea of standing by Bryce.

So what the hell is Jane even thinking? She's readjusting our places in line, over and over, literally by an inch. It's so annoying!

I might be hating Liam, but his daughter, Sophia, is cute as hell. She's running around my wild grass yard with her mom and a few other witches not in the wedding party, holding my fat gray cat, Whiskers. The cat is nearly half her size.

Liam switches with Bryce.

"You have the ring, Kates?" Maddie asks. She's right behind me, standing beside my brother.

"Yes, Maddie. I said I did a hundred times. We should have done this without formal clothes. And maybe with a fake ring." I glance at Liam's black sports jacket and slacks. "And the boys without suits."

"Mom wanted our practice to be perfect," Maddie says with a shrug. "I think she was worried we'd wear dark gothic clothes, and she wanted to practice "normal" for your dad. I'm just happy you came, Kate. I know how you feel about it."

It's funny, Maddie and I are so close, but this is like the first time she even mentioned me attending the wedding since my jab during Bryce's lecture the other day. I barely even talked about it with Dad. It's like my whole family figured that meeting with Damie was enough for me to accept their marriage. It really isn't. I still feel uncomfortable.

"Just make sure your mom makes this her *last* rehearsal," I say.

I hear a grunt. Liam glances over, furrowing his brow. But then I feel a real hard slap on my back.

"Ow!" I say, cocking my head. "Shit, that hurt, Maddie."

"So did those words, Cadence. So did the words. I know what you meant."

"Maybe I just meant this would be the last time practicing today?"

"Sure. Or the last time down the aisle, bitch."

"Well, I'm here. Okay?"

"That's why I was thanking you, *sister*."

I whirl around. Did you catch that? She said *sister*. She doesn't mean *sister* as in fellow witch, she means *sister* as in future sister, after Dad marries her mom.

"Don't ever call me that," I say. "Even after the wedding."

"How about *sister-in-law* after I marry your brother?"

Mira hears that one and bursts out laughing. Liam laughs too.

"Girls, come on," Jane says in front of the line. She's checking how straight everyone is standing. "If you have too much fun down there, you won't keep straight, Mira. I'm almost ready."

"Come on, Jane!" cries Mira. "Hurry this up."

"Then don't move, Mira," Jane says.

"You want to start a fight on my hallowed ground, Black-bird?" I ask, cocking my head back.

"You wouldn't want to cast against your own family, sis," Damien says.

"Shut up, Damie!" I snap. "Don't you start too."

"Come on, let's not fight," Liam says quickly. But he's holding back laughter.

Aunt Jane is moving bodies. It's so stupid. Now she's moving one of my cousins to the front of the line.

We stop talking. Not because I'm ever going to listen to pervert-creep beside me, but because we started out trading jabs for fun. Maddie and I know how far to take fooling around. But, really, another dig and this might turn into an actual fight between us.

"Glad you could come, Liam," Maddie says, touching him lightly on the shoulder. Did she just say that because she knows Liam and I are fighting too?

"Cadence?" Liam asks, staring ahead as Aunt Jane keeps rearranging bridesmaids. "Tell me about this witch, Enora. What are you guys planning to do to stop her attack?"

"I'm surprised you never met her. Alondra never mentioned her before?"

He shakes his head.

Whatever.

I don't believe him. Look, you have to understand that there is no man I ever hated in this world more than his *best friend* Will Reardon. I always saw Reardon as the true ringleader of perversion here in Hawthorne. I will never get over what Reardon did to Maddie. Not to mention Reardon transformed me into a snake. Not to mention, especially, that I'm standing by a man who did the same pervert spells to innocent girls at Hawthorne University.

"You're still upset with me?" he asks rhetorically.

Yep. I sure am. But I mumble, "No."

"You make a bad liar." He chuckles. "It reminds me of someone I know."

"Alondra?"

"No, me," he says, shaking his head. "Tell me what you're planning to do about Enora so I can help, Cadence."

"I don't want your help. You're not even willing to practice magic."

"Okay," shouts Jane. "Mira, Courtney, you guys ready back there? Maddie? Cadence? We're all going to walk in single file and then separate near the logs here. Bryce, you're going to walk with me for now. We're—"

"Cadence, when are you planning the séance?" Liam insists. "Jane and I want to help."

Is he for real?

"Enora can enter our dreams," Maddie says. "She's done it before. That's what we're all worried about."

"We're worried Enora's going to attack us, Mr. Johansen," Damien adds.

Aunt Jane takes Bryce out of line again for a second. What the hell is she doing? She's really obsessed with this line for some reason. Is this a wedding jitters thing? I mean, I was nervous before my wedding, but I didn't act this crazy...or maybe I did. But I hadn't gotten married a thousand times before either.

Dad pulls her aside. It's so typical of my shy dad, preferring to talk to her more discreetly. I think he's getting tired of all this too.

Liam's looking at me still. What the hell was he asking again?

"I have to get your wife out of my head," I say to Liam. "We have to try, or, I tell you, I'm going to go star-craving mad."

"The expression is stark-raving mad, dummy," Maddie says behind me, laughing. "But yours fits witches better."

"Shut it, Maddie. Liam's right, we don't need to fight."

"Only one fighting around here is you, bitch."

"Sounds like you need to get rid of Enora *and* Alondra," Liam says.

"Are you sure I'm not dream casting without knowing it?" I

ask him. "Couldn't spirits inside me be using me to attack Enora and her friends?"

"She already cursed and attacked you, Kates," Maddie interjects.

"I'm asking our expert warlock."

"Jane told me all about Enora," Liam says. "I heard what she did to you and Madison. I agree you have to do something about her. One of the reasons you're suffering so much, I think, is Alondra passed too early. She should have helped you get through all of this white versus dark magic. It's part of being the High Priestess in Hawthorne under my wife's legacy, I think." Then he looks deeply in my eyes. He frowns. "Some aspects of dark conjurings can be used for good. Even Agnes conceded to that, and she devoted her life to right-sided magic. Only someone like you, with your heart, like Agnes before she passed, can do this right. That's why you lead this town. Alondra and I and my friend, who you hated, failed.

"I'm not only a retired witch, I'm also a counselor. I see how much this stuff is tearing you apart. The truth is, I might have lied when we fought at Jane's house. I didn't only come here to walk Jane down the aisle, I came here to help you too."

"That's so nice, Mr. Johansen," says Maddie, touching his shoulder.

"Shut up, Maddie," I say, whirling around.

Maddie sticks her tongue out at me. But I'm not hating Liam so much now. But then I think, *wait!* This man brought Professor Reardon here to Hawthorne! I mean, *Reardon!*

Goety, goety, goety.

"I believe Allie is inside you," Liam says, "because it wasn't enough for Kenosha to stay and help. Not even giving you *Broomstick* was enough. Jane and I can accompany your séance, if you'll have us. I'll do whatever I can to help get Allie out of you.... If you'll have us. We want to help you."

"You'll cast magic?"

"For you, and only you, Cadence, yes. Your success means protecting your friends. That means Maddie and even Jane. And even your brother here and your dad. I ask you to let me go to your ceremony, not just for me, but for them."

And he looks into my eyes with such care. It's almost hypnotic. Is he casting some warlock spell on me? Or does he genuinely care about me? For a second, I like him again.

Let me see my husband one last time, Cadence. Please. Don't forgive Lee or me? Fine. But just let me see him before I pass on.

Pass on? What the hell? If you're planning on leaving, why even have this séance? You're leaving, Alondra?

After ceremony.

"Are you ready to walk down the aisle with me, Lee?" Jane asks. "Talked with Cadence enough?"

Her words break his gaze from mine. I practically jump in surprise. I didn't see Jane come over, but she is standing right next to us.

"We've been waiting, Mom," Maddie says. "I think they finally had enough time to hash things out. But now she and I are fighting."

"We're not fighting," I say.

"Well, let's get on with it," Jane says with a smirk. Then she taps Bryce. "Bryce, you switch back with Liam. Liam, you're going to be the one taking me down the aisle. You know that."

"Jane!" I say. "You shuffled us around just so I'd talk to him?"

"Whatever do you mean, Cadence?" Jane asks.

"Jane was never a great liar either," Liam quips with a chuckle.

"Come on, Lee," Jane says, taking his arm in hers. "We're going to the back. You need to practice taking me down the aisle to marry Cadence's amazing father."

Bryce takes my hand and stands beside me again. He nods and smiles. But then...

Mira rushes out of line. And Courtney runs too. What the

hell? Everyone's breaking Jane's precious line. I furrow my brow and turn toward our patio. It's Frida! My sweetest friend is standing, all smiley, with her blond-haired future hubby, Greg! They're both totally casual in T-shirts and jeans. I think I hear Jane say something, but it's too late. We're all rushing out of line now. And my backyard is long. It takes me forever to end up in Frida's arms.

"Oh, Katie," Frida says, with a laugh, in my arms. "I've missed you."

"I missed you so much, Frida, you don't even know," I say, running my hand in her hair. "You guys here long?"

"For the wedding, Katie," Frida says with a nod. "Yes. For your dad and Aunt Jane."

"I haven't been in Hawthorne since *your* wedding, Cadence," Greg says with a smile and nod. Greg hasn't changed much. He's a tall, lanky guy with a thin beard.

"Hi Greg. Make yourselves at home, guys," I say. "I'm so glad you came."

I really am. And Frida looks so happy to see us.

"Hey, Freeds!" yells Maddie.

Looking back, I see Aunt Jane, Liam, and my dad walking slowly toward us. There must be thirty people in my backyard, and they're all converging around my sweet friend. Pamela is even ushering Sophie over. Then Frida makes me laugh. She seems so bashful amid all the attention. She's such a shy girl.

After a few hundred more greetings, I'm surprised to see a bald dark-skinned woman shake Frida's hand. Kenosha. When did she get here?

"Hi, Doctor Trent," Frida says, hugging her. Then she flashes a rueful grin at me. "Is it still hard, Katie?"

"Very," Kenosha says to Frida. "I'm not only here for the wedding."

"Okay, okay," Aunt Jane says, clapping loudly. "Enough. Come on. So, it's so great to see you, Frida, thanks so much for coming and please come watch us, but, come on everyone. Let's just finally walk down this aisle and get this over with."

"Stand by us," Maddie says to Frida, guiding her back into the line. "If I had known you were in town, I'm sure Kates and I would have had you in the ceremony."

"I'm just happy to watch, Maddie," Frida says.

"Frida," Mira says, grabbing her arm, "how about you, me, Maddie, and Katie here just play hooky inside for the rest of this rehearsal?"

"Get back in line, Meer," Courtney says, rolling her eyes.

And we laugh.

16

PARLEY IN THE PARLOR

I'M SITTING BESIDE BESTIE NUMBER TWO—YOU KNOW, FRIDA—ON this peach vinyl booth, swirling my favorite mix of caramel and fudge with a large spoon while taking in the nice view of the foggy street. It's real overcast outside. Through the large window, I can barely make out the trees on the other side of the one-way road.

A student rides past on a bike.

Frida is quietly spooning some delicious goo. This impromptu lunch-dessert meeting is pretty much the complete opposite of the last time we met here at Hawthorne Sweets. Back then, Frida was barely talking to me, and I was acting crazy under a witch's dark curse.

Frida sure seems to be enjoying her Caramel Apple Surprise this time. A delightful bright red sauce is dripped over vanilla ice cream and an adorable cinnamon stick hangs from the side. She's all smiles. I just love her.

"So, when's the date, Frida?" I ask, licking more chocolate ice cream while biting into a small chocolate chip.

"Greg and I aren't sure, Katie," she replies with a laugh. "He wants to work things out with his job in New York."

"What's he doing again?"

"Graphic design."

"How about you? Did you get a teaching job?"

"Not yet. I'm taking a break."

Then she dips some of that cinnamon stick in the red sauce and vanilla ice cream.

"May I?" I ask with a raised spoon.

She nods and pushes her bowl a little closer.

I swirl my spoon in her vanilla ice cream. But the real treat is the red sauce. It's actually warm along my tongue, like hot fudge. And it's super sweet, like my friend, with an apple-y taste. Added to the apple is just the perfect chili spice kick that makes it absolutely delicious.

Hawthorne Sweets is so surreal. All of our university buildings are made of brick and mortar and were built over a hundred years ago. Not Hawthorne Sweets. This ice cream parlor is all glass, fashioned like a hamburger diner. Two large ice cream statues stand by the entrance. The walls are peach and pink. And there's a parlor bar with 1950 swivel chairs. The waiters and waitresses walk about in peach or pink aprons wearing diner caps. Most of the tabletops are metallic silver, and there are multicolored place mats. It's like totally surreal. It's such a rainbow of pastel colors in the middle of our green and brown forest. So weird. But so wonderful. I think that's why so many students love it here too.

A girl traipses by outside with a bag full of books slung over her shoulder. She's wearing a skirt and a red and gold Hawthorne University sweater.

"This is really good, Katie," Frida says. "You were right."

"Got that right, Freeds," I say with a nod. "So?" I ask again with a yawn.

"So *what* Katie?"

"So...when's the date, Frida? Come on, I think you've been hanging with Greg longer than any of us. I mean, there's no rush, you know, I just want to watch you go down the aisle together." She laughs. "Or maybe I just want to be invited to your wedding."

"You sound like Bryce," Frida says with a laugh, touching my shoulder. "I don't care as long as Greg and I are together. But when we do it, you'll be the first one to be invited."

"I know. But when?"

"What about this?" Frida asks, rubbing my belly. It's just starting to protrude. "Did the doctor confirm it's a baby girl, like you foresaw?"

"Yeah. Chandra. I told you. Maybe that's the other reason I wanted to come here? Maybe Chandra wanted ice cream."

Frida nods with a laugh. But then she opens her eyes wide in surprise, examining my eyes. I almost cover them, afraid they're changing green.

"What?" I ask. "They're still brown, right?"

"No, you've got such rings under your eyes. Aren't you sleeping? You need to sleep for the baby."

"I know." I yawn again. Boy, am I tired. "Bitch-witch isn't letting any of us sleep. Bryce and I take turns watching each other at night, ready to wake the other if we stir too much from a nightmare. The whole coven's totally on edge. Has she been haunting you?"

"No." She sighs. "There's always trouble in Hawthorne, especially with you as leader. It's not your fault, but it's been so bad for you. That's why I ran." She shows a rueful grin. "I feel so horrible for that, but I—"

"I know, Frida, forget it," I say, raising my palm. "Look, I can barely take it either." Then I put an arm around her again. "Just don't leave me again, okay?"

"You need all of us," she says with a nod. "Alondra made you responsible for not only this town, but all of your friends. I heard about Mira's séance. You know I've given up being a witch, I can't be there for magic, but, if you want, I can still be there for you. Maybe Mira can help?"

"It's up to you," I say, dipping my chocolatey spoon in more luscious caramel. A whole spoonful. "You're welcome to. I hope Mira can do it. Kenosha will be there to try to help."

"Where are you going to do it?"

"Kenosha came up with the Billington House. She suggested it because it's Abigail's ancient home. But I've been confusing Abigail with Alondra. So it could get pretty hairy. But it's better than my house, we think. We don't want Alondra coming out of me and haunting the house again. Remember when all our lights used to turn on by themselves? Trouble is, we're going to have to sneak into the Billington House. Bryce's fraternity even wanted to use the place for Halloween, but it hasn't passed inspection. But if Kenosha thinks that house is the place to perform the ceremony, I'm in. Liam and Jane will be there. And so will our entire coven."

"Maybe I should go," Frida says with a nod. But she sounds so unsure. "When?"

"Friday, of course. Do you remember, a long time ago, when I ran out of the Billington House fighting with Maddie a few years ago?" But then, I can't recall if she was there. "Mira was running a séance, but she was using a plastic toy Ouija board and I barely even knew who she was. I hadn't been initiated yet. Anyway, Mira didn't even know she had succeeded with my mom. My mom, who had passed a couple hours before the séance, sent me a personal message. It was scary, but beautiful. My mom simply said, "I love you." Then her name came up on the board. Anyway, it was also creepy, but the point is, Mira's got a lot more ghost summoning power than she thinks. And so maybe—yeah, maybe—Mira can get this ghost out of me Friday. And then Bryce and I, and all of our sisters, will be able to sleep again."

"I sure hope so, Katie," she says, touching my arm. "I really hope so."

And that's when a shadow is cast over our table. At first, I'm thinking it's our waitress again, but then I see Frida's frightened expression. Standing over her is Enora! And Cordelia is by her side. But that's not all. They both look so fucking weird, wearing scarlet robes and thick black gothic makeup.

"Oh, hi, Katie. Mind if we join you?"

Enora doesn't wait for my expletives. They're already sitting across from us. Cordelia folds her arms and gives a nasty, disgusting smirk. She's wearing a bunch of gaudy gold necklaces and about five earrings on each ear. Her face was already weird enough with her cheeks and forehead covered in dark magic sigils and demon drawings. And she's about two times the size of her bitch leader, Enora. Enora's face is very beautiful, as usual, in her loathsome smugness. Enora scrunches her nose, glancing at Frida.

"So, you're both history majors, right?" Enora asks, leaning forward. "Do you know about parleys? A parley is when two enemies meet with one another in the center of the battlefield before battle."

"*Get out of here, Enora!*" I exclaim, slamming my palms on the table. Then I look at Frida, getting angrier. Frida looks so scared. "*You planning on crashing another one of my cars! You know this is my hallowed ground.*"

"If you were a true witch, properly schooled in our arts, Katie, you'd know that there are ways around rules like that. All rules are made to be broken, particularly when we wise women spend time in careful preparation. But that's your whole problem. See, as much as you hate me, right now Cordelia and all her friends hate you so much more."

"Sure do, master," Cordelia adds, nodding with nasty smugness.

Another shadow passes over Frida. But this one is our innocent young waitress in her peach dress.

"Would you two like to order something?" the waitress asks Cordelia, pointing to laminated menus leaning on a silver napkin box.

Enora's smile widens. She picks up the single-page menu.

"Oh yes," Enora says in a really weird childish voice, pointing. "Can you get me a triple-scoop strawberry ice cream sundae? I'd just love it."

Cordelia bursts into laughter and rocks back and forth like an idiot, guffawing way too hard.

The waitress furrows her brow.

"Do you serve absinthe, miss?" Enora asks in her normal infernal voice, "How 'bout whiskey? Chartreuse?"

The waitress shakes her head. Then she seems to get the hint from Enora's silence. The waitress walks off, looking confused.

"Get out of here," I repeat, standing up.

A gust of wind shakes the glass window. And another shadow follows. This time it's the clouds obscuring the sun, turning an already overcast day as dark as night. Cordelia loses all her smugness and shakes. My magic is causing Frida to shake too.

Enora scowls. Then she squints her eyes.

"Parley for the parlor, Cadence," Enora says, raising a finger. "Parley for the parlor. Parley, not fight. Anyways—" She points at Frida. "It's not proper to cast spells in front of zealots. I hear you're not a witch anymore, Frida? Turned Catholic?"

Cordelia laughs again.

"Leave her alone!" I snap.

"Katie already hurled you across our lawn," snaps Frida. "You want her to do it again?"

"Actually, I was kind of hoping to witness a miracle from

your god," Enora says. "If you're such a believer, why don't you show me some of his magic."

There's a flash of light and a crack of lightning.

"Parley, Windstorm," Enora says, putting her hand up. It's that shriveled, scarred right hand I once burned in a fire. "Parley in the ice cream parlor."

"How do you know that was from me?"

"Look," Enora says, heaving a sigh, "when I wrecked Allie's car, I tried to reach you in the nonmagical way. Just like you reached out and called me. Excessively." She reaches down into her cloak, rummaging through pockets. She brings out her phone and runs a finger along the screen, showing me a list of numbers. "You called my phone about thirty times. Want to see? Well, here I am. Let's talk. This is not oneiromancy, witches. We're wide awake. So what did you want to talk about, my dear Hawthorne *friend*?"

"How about discussing how you're fucking leaving Hawthorne."

"She's so rude, master," Cordelia says, shaking her head and smiling wide.

"Sure is," Enora says with her own fake smile. "Why not sit down? I said this is a parley, not a fight."

"And I said, get the fuck out." And I point at the front door.

The lady and a man in a matching peach uniform working behind the counter are staring at us.

"Okay, look," Enora says, standing up, raising her left palm this time. That's the one with her stupid black upside-down pentacle. I'm not sure which one bothers me more.

Then gargantuan gorilla Cordelia stands up too. That gets my dear friend Frida to also stand. We're all standing. But Frida's short, about half Cordelia's size.

"I came to ask another favor of you," Enora says, "but honestly, Katie, I deplore asking you favors. You know why? As evil as you claim me to be, you're never nice responding to any of my simple requests."

"*What!?*"

"I'd like to accompany you during your upcoming séance. Think of it as a peace offering. I want to help. I have as much interest in fixing Hawthorne as you do. And, next to you, I'm the most powerful witch around."

"You're kidding?"

"She's not kidding, bitch," says Cordelia. "Master is the most powerful magus—"

"I meant, stupid, that your master must be kidding that she wants to join us. Why do you call her master, anyway? Are you her dog?"

Cordelia literally snarls at me as if to prove it. But then Enora puts her infernal hand up again and signals for Cordelia to sit down.

Cordelia broods. But she doesn't stop glaring. Then Cordelia flicks her fingers at my face and says: "*Serpentus cadere. Cadere. Cadere.*"

A rush of air around me hurls me back down into the booth.

"*Stand down, Adder!*" Enora cries.

"We need to fight, master!" shouts Cordelia. "She needs to be stopped, not talked to!"

"*Vade retro, satana!*" says Frida. Then she clutches the crucifix on her neck. Cordelia is hurled back down into the booth too.

The two workers are staring with wide eyes. So are a couple and a family a few booths down. But the workers don't approach. I think they're more weirded out than concerned about our fighting. None of us have even laid a finger on each other yet.

"Well, well, well," Enora says with a laugh, sitting back down, "surprise, surprise, Frida. I wonder if her belief in Jesus

Christ wills her god's power from the cross? I never thought she had any magic in her at all."

"You're next to fall, bitch!" I cry.

"Invite me to your coven's ceremony," Enora says, "and all the bickering ends. We want the same thing—even my dear friend Adder wants it. Sleep. No more nightmares. Nice dreams and nice sleep. That's it. No more fighting. Just invite me—"

"If you invite her, Katie," Frida says, "she'll be empowered on your hallowed ground. Then she can trick you again."

"But you've trusted me with my magic before," Enora objects. "You let me blindfold you to empower you against the Samhain Witch. You and I are now linked in magic under Selene. We, together, can give Hawthorne peace. Besides, I'm assuming you're inviting Madison's mom, that old green witch, and Alondra's wicked first husband, Allie's warlock? I can't fight all of you. You all can take me on if things go awry. I can't trick you with those old geezers. I can't take you all on. And it's your hallowed ground, isn't it? So? What do you say? A truce, witches?"

I look at Frida. She shakes her head vehemently.

"Okay," I say with a nod.

Enora squints her eyes. So does Cordelia. So does Frida. They don't believe me.

"But you owe me for my car."

"That was never your car," Enora says with a laugh. "But if I can help bring peace to Hawthorne and—" She points to my stomach. "You and Bryce's future, I think I will have made enough amends. Don't you?" Then she looks down at Frida. "Except maybe Frida. Frida's completely hopeless."

"Let's go, Frida," I say, getting up again. "I've suddenly lost my appetite."

"Don't bother," Enora says, throwing her hood over her head. "We'll go. I don't want to disturb your joy in eating ice cream." She looks at Adder and nods toward the exit. "Thanks so much for the invitation, Windstorm. I'm so looking forward to our little soiree."

"I didn't tell you where it will be held."

"We'll see you at the Billington House this Friday, Cadence."

Then Frida and I watch them walk to the exit. They don't look back. But as the hooded red witches rush past our window on the sidewalk, I hear Enora say, "Blessed be, bitches." Then her stupid lackey laughs like a hyena.

17

RAVEN'S SÉANCE

THE TABLE FOR OUR SÉANCE IS MADE UP OF FIVE PLASTIC FOLD-out tables connected together. I know because I watched my friends connect them. But you'd never know it. The witches running this show, Kenosha and Mira, covered everything with a silky purple velvet cloth decorated in pentagrams and stars. Lying on the tablecloth are all kinds of other witchy stuff: tarot cards, candles, crystals, burning incense, crystal balls, runes, and human bones. It smells of frankincense. I'm dead center. Mira's sitting across from me beside Kenosha. Kenosha's bald in her forest-green robe, and Mira's in her pitch-black robe. To my left, a few seats away, sit our archenemy bitches Enora and Cordelia, wearing scarlet. I try not to look at them. The love of my life is to my right and my BFF, Maddie, is to my left. We're wearing our black robes. A few chairs down from Bryce are Liam and Aunt Jane—Liam's in black like us, and Jane is in light green. Other invited guests in black include Josie, Debra, Chandra, Beth, Nancy, and Noori. Basically, *everyone* in my entire coven is here. Mira's girlfriend, Courtney, is sitting beside her opposite Kenosha. Even Frida's here, standing by the door, in a T-shirt and burying her hands in her jeans pockets. With the crowds, you'd think the room would be noisy. It's not. It's unusually quiet with everyone intently staring at me, waiting.

Willow keeps waving incense over the table in front of me, closing her eyes, bowing her head, and murmuring weird stuff I don't even know about. Even though it's technically Mira's séance, Kenosha's roots are as a voodoo witch, deep into this necromancy stuff. So Willow might belong here more than Mira. And necromancy is all about what we're doing. We're summoning the dead.

A Geiger counter by the entryway seems exceptionally loud. Enora looks over occasionally with disgust, probably wondering who brought that gadget to our séance. That'd be Raymond. He's the only person, aside from Frida and his daughter, Cat, who's wearing "normal" clothes. Cat is standing beside him. Remember her? She's that fun young girl with the weirdest hairdo—bald on one side, pigtails on the other. She's transfixed by us, waiting for something to happen. Even though she isn't a witch, I think she likes this stuff as much as Mira does. Cat called me last week talking about getting into college. She wanted to know about Hawthorne, and, when I blabbed stupidly about the séance we're having, there was absolutely no way she wouldn't come. Me and my big mouth. The Geiger counter is an EMF detector to catch ghosts. They have also set up a really weird small black box that's playing static.

"Okay, Cadence," Mira says. She looks into my eyes. Under the flickering yellow candlelight, she's creepy. "Are you ready?"

"I think everybody is ready."

"Séances are more spectacle than real magic," Kenosha says with a nod, "but if we hold hands, with enough magical intent, the spirits may still come. This room was chosen as it's been decided that it is safer than holding ceremony at your house. Alondra's old house. Being on both Abigail's and Escoba's hallowed ground, this building should have the most direct connection with your ancestors, while diminishing the power of your teacher. This house became Escoba's after all. If Alondra is a spirit, and not a demon as I've proposed, she should appear. And, perhaps, Escoba will as well." She looks around our long rectangular table. "Now, please, everyone, look at the person beside you. We are occult. Make sure that your neighbor is schooled in our craft and we have no outsiders here."

"The only non-witches in the room are the ghost hunters," Bryce says beside me. He gestures at Raymond and Cat by the door. "But Raymond worked with Alondra's ghost haunts for decades. They're not witches, but they know ghosts."

"I saw magic last time I was with Cadence." Cat smiles at me. "She made a boy levitate over a couch. It was so incredibly dope."

"No one will talk, Willow," I say. "But, Cat—" I glance over. "Absolutely no recording or photography, okay?"

"Come on, Cadence," Cat objects.

I smile at her and shake my head. I can just imagine the temptation.

"It's hard to believe, with so many people, that everyone can be trusted," Kenosha says.

"Thank Alondra for that," I say. "She brought us all together."

"Actually, Alondra's mother was a witch," Kenosha objects.

"The only people who shouldn't be here are my friends," Bryce says. "They're by the front door. I can't very well keep members of the fraternity out of their own house."

"Very well, High Priest," Kenosha says with a nod. "Very well. Blessed be."

Kenosha reaches under the table and carefully places a skull in front of me. Then she reaches under the table again and brings up something covered in a violet cloth—a similar color to the cloth over the table. She smiles. Lifting the cloth, she reveals a small crystal ball. This one can fit in her palm, but it has lines and cracks inside it, making it look damaged, unlike the huge crystal ball, about twice its size, right in front of me. She hands me the small orb, but...honestly, I can't stop looking at the skull.

"Is that a real skull?" I ask, pointing at it.

"Of course it is," Kenosha says with a nod. "I can tell you who it is, if you'd like."

People laugh. Very funny, Kenosha. Of course, although she's chuckling, she's probably telling the truth.

"Cadence," Kenosha says, "notice two large amethyst crystals before you on either side of the large glass ball. One to your right and one to your left. The large glass ball on the table, unlike the quartz in your hand, is for show, but all the orbs, even that one, draw energy from the amethyst crystals. Purple is a very powerful conjuring color."

"That must be why I keep seeing it in visions?"

Kenosha shrugs.

"The crystal quartz ball you hold in your hand now," Kenosha says, "is a special gift from my Crescent Coven. My good friend and current High Priestess, Clotho, gives this offering from my coven back in New Orleans. It is very old. Many believe it might have even belonged to our blessed sister Marie Laveau, two hundred years ago. Or, perhaps, even Escoba laid hands on this when she was a part of my coven. We trace much of our root work back to these great mambo witches."

"Thanks," I say.

"Now lay the crystal ball back on the table. Its energy will enhance Raven's magic."

Then she opens a small leather pouch and pours dirt all over the small crystal ball.

"Why are you getting such a pretty thing dirty?" asks Beth, sitting by Nancy.

"This is grave dirt, Beth," Kenosha says. "It will ground the energy of the quartz. Whatever happens around the table,

Cadence, if we lose connection, this orb will serve as protection and as a bridge from the spirit world to ours."

"I prefer obsidian," Enora says.

"Crystal is better," Kenosha argues, shaking her head. "Particularly this valuable quartz. This is pure quartz, Cadence."

"Can we get on with this, Willow?" Enora asks in a huff. "I mean, I would think the High Priestess of the Hawthorne coven would know what the fuck a crystal ball is." Cordelia laughs. "Katie, all this pomp is *your* show. You're running this coven, not weeping willow. Adder and I, from the Abaddon coven of Atlanta, also protect you with our blessed presence." Cordelia cackles again. "Now, can we fucking get on with it?"

"We had to wait for all her nice friends, master," quips Cordelia.

"Aha," Enora says. "Sure did."

"You two shouldn't even be here," snaps Maddie.

"Really, Blackbird, only real witches should be in ceremony," Enora replies with a nod. "You probably should leave."

"What makes you think you're a real witch?" asks Aunt Jane.

"Come on, stop fighting, guys," I say. "Enora's here by my invitation. And she's right, we need to get on with it, Kenosha. Please."

"Thank you, Katie," Enora says.

"Mira has studied séances more than I have, Windstorm," Kenosha says with a nod to Mira. "And so, Raven shall preside."

"Everyone hold hands," Mira says. She closes her eyes. "Windstorm, you are the leader of the Hawthorne coven. However, I have studied séances for years. With your permission, and Willow's consent, I will run this ceremony."

"Are we going to spend another hour requesting permission?" asks Enora. Cordelia laughs again.

"She really is annoying," Liam says. "You were so right, Cadence."

"Whatever did Falconsong see in you, warlock?" asks Enora.

"Just stop it, guys!" I cry. "Go on, Mira. Just go."

"Hand me Willow's, or...your, crystal ball, Windstorm," Mira says.

I hand it across the table to her.

"Now everyone," Mira says, looking into the orb. "Everybody sitting around this table, we shall chant our wish. We wish to summon the spirits of Escoba, Abigail, and Alondra. I will consider evoking any one of these spirits a success. And any one of these spirits can help end Windstorm's possession—even if it be an Ekimmu, Willow. Repeat the following words with all your magical intent."

Then she places my small crystal ball on the table before us. She closes her eyes, bobs her head up and down, breathes real hard, and runs her fingers over my crystal ball. She's looking a bit ridiculous. It's like when she summoned my mom a few years ago. But Kenosha has her eyes shut and is nodding with intense focus. So are Liam and Aunt Jane. And Bryce and Maddie. Even Frida, standing by the door, closes her eyes and nods. Everyone is focusing on getting rid of you, Alondra.

"Wait," says Cat.

We all stop and look up.

"Wait, Cadence." Cat's words sound so jarring. "Shouldn't we pour salt around your table? Isn't that part of the ceremony with the candles, to create a space for the magic to work?"

"Shh, Cat," I say. "Not now."

"Are you a witch?" Mira asks, annoyed.

"She's a ghost hunter," I say.

"*Ghost hunter*," Mira says contemptuously. "I would ask that you don't interrupt us again. Please stay quiet or leave."

"But, I mean...should we, Mira?" I ask. "Is she right?"

Mira just scowls.

"Limestone, or salt, can keep spirits from reaching all the witches around the table," Kenosha explains to Cat and the newbies. "But as witches, we hold enough energy to deal with any spirits. But I advise you and your father to stay by the door, outsider. And, I suppose, there's nothing wrong with *you* sprinkling salt around—"

"*Fuck!*" cries Enora. "*Get on with it! This isn't a goddamn class!*"

"Enora!" I snap. "Shut up."

Enora seethes, clenching her teeth. She heaves a sigh, throws her long hair back, and then flashes a very fake grin. "Pardon me, High Priestess of Hawthorne, please, please continue your ceremony."

Mira nods. Then she closes her eyes again.

I put a finger over my lips to shush Cat.

"*Spiritus, spiritus,*" Mira says. "*Spiritus. Come forth. Venite foras.* We call on you in the house of Josiah Billington. We ask that Mr. Billington's wife and the slave Escoba Hawthorne appear before us. We also ask that our revered former leader and High Priestess, Alondra Johansen, materialize here before us. Come forth, spirits. Come from the Summerland. We invite you here. The revered High Priestess of the Hawthorne coven invites you. Windstorm, Willow, Blackbird, Raven, Panthera, and Owl Jay invite you. The High Wizards Liam Johansen and Bryce Wallace invite you. All great witches of Hawthorne call on you, spirits. Spirits *venite foras. Venite. Venite.*"

Venite foras. Venite. Venite.

"And now," Mira says, opening her eyes and looking at all of us, "everyone repeat these names: Abigail... Escoba... Alondra. Their names themselves shall evoke their presence."

"*Abigail... Escoba... Alondra.*"

We repeat the names over and over.

I open an eye and peek. Everybody's saying their names with their eyes closed in concentration, even Enora and Cordelia.

"*Abigail, Escoba, Alondra.*"

But I don't feel magic.

"*Abigail, Escoba, Alondra.*"

Nothing's happening.

No...wait... I hear words. They're not only spoken by everyone around the table, they're spoken quietly in that weird black box Raymond brought over. But it's too faint to discern, and the words are cut up by static. Raymond and Cat hear it. Our ghosthunters get real excited, crouching down and turning up the volume of the box.

"*Abigail, Escoba, Alondra,*" the machine says between static.

"Come forth," Mira repeats, more excitedly, "yes, come forth upon these grounds. The house of Escoba. The house of Abigail. The house of Alondra Billington. And the house of Cadence Hawthorne. Repeat it once more, everyone: Abigail, Escoba, Alondra."

Anu... Ereshkigal... Inanna.

Anu, Ereshkigal, Inanna.

Anu, Ereshkigal, Inanna.

I open my eyes and feel a surge of fear. Mira and Kenosha are gone. So are Maddie and Bryce, who were sitting beside me. Everyone's gone. I'm sitting alone at the center of the long table. A dim violet light flickers along the empty walls and concrete flooring of our large room. The table, which displayed so many magical trinkets, is completely void of nearly everything except candles. All the candles shine violet instead of yellow. Before me are my book, *Broomstick,* and that lovely small crystal ball Kenosha gifted me.

I take my quartz ball into my palms.

But I'm not alone.

In my reflection in the magical orb, I see tall, dark, lanky figures behind me, nearly tall enough to touch the ceiling. They are armless, without discernible faces, with glowing white eyes.

I've never seen an Ekimmu, but this is the image once described by Alondra in our circle. And, now that I think of it, I saw them crouched over that strange goblin-like creature, that Alu, in my recent wandering. Was Kenosha right all along? Are these demons haunting me?

I spin around and see only my shadow on the wall in the flickering light. The spirits are gone. When I turn back, there's no one in the room. But then, gazing into the crystal ball again, through smoky purple wisps of smoke, I see their giant, lanky, faceless bodies in front of me. They're surrounding me, standing behind every empty chair, with those creepy white eyes. It's as if these demons are holding the séance. But I only see them reflected in or through the crystal ball.

I feel scared.

I jump up, but I trip trying to get out of my chair. I want to get the hell out of here. Then I hear a shrill, ear-piercing scream in the darkness. I throw Kenosha's velvet cloth over the ball in my hand.

"Windstorm," a voice says. It's Alondra, but it sounds like it's coming from everywhere.

I hear another shrill scream. It's so weird. I don't see the devils. I don't want to see them. But I hear them. The shrill cries are so high-pitched and loud that it hurts, as if someone's in intense pain or being tortured. It's like the legendary scream of the banshee.

Enora appears in her chair to my left—*only* Enora at an otherwise empty table. She has her head lowered and is chanting Mira's séance words again. It's weird. Then she turns, looks right into my eyes, and says, "I can manifest the evil among you. But I don't think you'll like it."

Enora disappears.

Then come those terrible banshee screams again.

"*Vade retro, diabolus,*" I snap, looking everywhere. "*Stop! Vade retro. This is my hallowed ground!*"

"Remove your blindfold, Cadence," says Alondra's voice. "Your initiation is over."

Blindfold? What blindfold?

She's right. Although I see the flickering candlelit room, I feel a blindfold over my eyes. Then I have this sudden freaky and creepy feeling. It's like grima again. What if I never awoke from Enora's spell? What if everything I've seen up to this point since my blindfold spell has been an illusion? What if I'm still in Meadow Park with Enora!

"Don't remove your blindfold," objects Enora's voice in my ear.

I cover my eyes and start crying under the blindfold. Because I'm afraid. I don't understand what's happening.

I shake my head. No. I don't want to remove the blindfold. I'm too scared. Tears are now streaming under the cloth and over my cheeks.

I'm okay. Everything is okay... right? You're still with me? Are you?

I take a deep breath.

That shining violet ball glows in my hands again. Did I remove the cloth over it? The purple is beautiful. This is the same purple glow I've been seeing for months.

I lift the quartz to my face, and now, through the glass, I see the shadows of my friends still sitting at the table. Their lips still chant the three names, but I don't hear them. And it's weird because my friends are transparent, as if they are the ghosts they're trying to summon. I can only see my friends as reflections in the ball. And yes, those horrible Ekimmu are still in the room, one is standing over each of my friends.

"Remove your blindfold, Windstorm," Alondra orders. "It's time."

"We arranged this ceremony for you to leave, Alondra!" I shout, looking around the dark, empty room. "Where are you? You have to leave!"

"Oh, I'll leave. I'll leave soon enough. Don't worry, selfish woman. But whether you wish to help me or not, Cadence, you're a part of my coven and you're still a witch. You're the Hawthorne Witch."

I don't see her. How can I? I still have the blindfold over my eyes.

All I see is the large table in an empty room with flickering candlelight—unless I look through the ball. The strangest thing, the thing that doesn't make any sense, is that this dark room is like a veil. Because when I see the Ekimmu in the orb, I also see my friends. When I turn from the orb, I am alone in darkness.

So I remove my blindfold.

18

TENEBRIS

I GASP… SOMEHOW I'M SITTING IN A CUSHIONED LOUNGE CHAIR IN a small dusty room. But I can't move my arms or legs. A stairway, thick with dust, leads to a door. The only light in the room is flickering violet candlelight emanating from the ceiling. The chair, with an intricate red and white floral design on its arms, seems very old. And resting upon my belly is the small crystal ball.

I see a reflection of myself coming down the wooden stairway. A younger Cadence walks down the stairs holding hands with a younger Bryce. Bryce is holding a candle in his other hand, and the flickering yellow light guides their way. How could I forget this? This was when Bryce and I had our first kiss! I love this memory.

But my hubby doesn't pay any attention to me in the chair. He's paying attention to the "Cadence" standing by him in the small basement. We didn't really know each other well yet.

Cadence opens a large wooden chest in front of me. She sneezes. Looking over her shoulder, I see what's inside. There's a violet scarf and black dress caked in thick dust. She sneezes again. Then Cadence picks up a portrait. I recognize this photo.

It's a picture of me as a little girl opening a large red velvet box beside a Christmas tree. I must only be about six years old—the gift is as big as I am. But the photo frame looks about two hundred years old.

There's more. She looks at a baby photo. It's my cute little brother, Damie. I recognize a few photos from our old house in California. We moved to Atlanta when I turned seven, and I grew up there. But I don't think I've ever seen some of the other pictures. There's a cute photo of me sitting beside my younger brother reading him a bedtime story. The book I'm holding is the size of my chest. That's so cute. Another picture shows me pushing Damie on a three-wheeler. And then there's Dad in the forest, surrounded by huge red trees the size of cars. I'm thinking it's the Redwoods? I don't recall ever going to the Redwoods. Maybe I was there as a baby? It's like a history of my whole life in that chest. And Bryce is enjoying just watching me rummage through all these pictures.

Cadence lifts the most distinctive picture. One that makes me want to cry—this time, not in fear but because it's sad. It's Mom. My real mom. My mom is there in my chest too.

I miss you so much, Mom...

Mom is painted wearing a long forest-green dress tapered midway down and draping over her legs. The dress is old, right out of the nineteenth century. And standing beside her is her best friend, Escoba, a dark-skinned woman in a long white dress and white cloth headdress. They were friends. They were the best of friends, remember? It's so sad.

"Can I kiss you on the lips, Cadence?"

Cadence walks, as if in a trance, before my chair and drops all the photographs on my lap by my violet crystal ball. Then she stands under Bryce and nods. She's on her tippy toes, and the couple kisses.

And that feels so good.

But then the couple disappears.

I run bloody fingers over the photos of my past. I'm staining them with sticky crimson, still wet from my belly. A tear from my eye drops on the photos, mixing tears with blood. Then I see that one photo in my hand is not a photograph. It's a very old, worn, folded piece of paper.

The letter reads "*For Escoba.*"

I unfold the letter and read:

Dearest Essie,

I sent Virgil to search for you. Some say you're over at Jessie M. Davis's Farm, though I spoke with Jessie and he's uncertain of your whereabouts. Where did you go? Some say you are free. Hopefully, by Astraeus, my negro finds you and you receive this desperate note.

First, allow me to share my greatest gratitude. Your root work worked! Harm did not befall him in the way I expected, but then few things under Selene ever do.

But now, I must ask for something more. This is difficult... It is with great regret that I tell you that my two sons, Adam and James, have fallen ill with consumption. Thank God, Hester and I have not been affected yet. Hester has only a mild cough, and I believe my little girl is strong enough to recover. But my boys are not faring well. The doctor says they might not survive. I'm not sure who to turn to, Essie. With the recent departure of their father, things have gotten so desperate for us.

And so, I implore you to send me another bag that can cure them. Make me a gris-gris. Please. Oh please, Essie, please, dearest friend, please help save my boys! I will pay you anything in sacrifice for another gris-gris. Just please, please, help heal my boys.

Know that your magic be true. You proved yourself, once more, to hold greater power than I do. The deed is done, all thanks to you, Escoba. Josiah is dead. Now I need your magic once more to heal my children.

With love and immense admiration,

Abigail Billington

. . .

I hear "Abigail" repeated over and over in the small room.

And then...*ow! Ow!* I feel horrible pain in my stomach. Oh, no. *Chandra!* I was so worried about attending ceremony with her growing inside me. Bryce even suggested that I not attend. Is she hurt?

Ow! My stomach hurts so bad!

I start crying from the intense searing pain in my stomach. It reminds me of those demon cries. It's so horrible.

I look down and red blood is soaking my long white night-gown. In the center of the darkest red, over my lower belly, is the head of a dagger. I'm no longer holding Kenosha's crystal ball, I'm holding the handle of a dagger.

Ow.

And the pain is...unbearable.

I hear those shrill screams. Then I see them. Hovering over me, those tall, lanky, dark demons gaze down on me. Their white eyes are shining, providing the only light in the darkness.

"So... Escoba killed herself, Alondra?"

A bright white light blinds me.

The pain is gone. And the lack of that horrible stabbing pain is so soothing, so wonderful.

I'm sitting in one of our outdoor plastic chairs before the logs of our bonfire in the wild grass. Bryce is sitting beside me, holding my hand. After all that darkness, under the bright rays of the yellow sun, it feels so nice to be in our yard. The blue sky just has a few wisps of white clouds above. And the air smells of the woods. There's a slight breeze flowing against my cheek. Bryce leans over and kisses my lips. Then he looks down.

Instead of holding that knife in my belly, I'm holding a

beautiful baby. Chandra. And my baby is just looking up at me. My baby's smiling.

"I think she's hungry, Cadence," Bryce says.

Bryce touches the baby's lips and lets her suck his finger.

I laugh.

Then I turn toward the trees.

I see a shadow approaching. I don't want to, I prefer just looking down at my baby under the midday sun, or even up at the clear blue sky. But there's a witch walking toward us. A witch in one of our black Druid cloaks with a hood over her head. The black robe looks so dark among all the shining yellow rays through the light green leaves and branches. Behind the witch's hood, I recognize her face. Alondra.

When she stands over Bryce, everything turns dark, as if the sun has been eclipsed. And yet, not even that truly shadows Bryce, Chandra, and me. It's those wraith-like creatures again, those banshee-like screaming creatures, those Ekimmu. A whole gang of demons stands behind my former teacher.

"I bring you gnosis," Alondra says.

My baby starts crying.

"Stay away from us."

"I bring you my final lesson, Cadence," Alondra says clearly. Too clearly. Unlike in the dreamscape, Alondra's really here.

"I never asked for you to teach me anything. I asked you to leave."

"You summoned me to appear before you in Mira's séance."

I start bouncing the baby to try to shush her. Chandra's so upset. But Bryce isn't disturbed. He just runs his fingers over the thin hair on our baby's head and leans down to kiss her.

"Just go away! I never wanted to be a witch, okay? How many times do I have to tell you that? Not after what you did to Maddie and Bryce. I joined your coven to be with friends."

"I never wanted to be your teacher."

"Kenosha said you planned for me to be here."

"No, Cadence," Alondra says, shaking her head. Then she actually smiles down on me. "I didn't even want to run a coven. Students came to me for my magic."

"And look what you did with it! You and your husband made them perform sex rituals!"

"I never made anyone do anything they weren't willing to do."

I hold my baby close, bouncing her on my leg. She's inconsolable.

"No, I remember that excuse. That's a lie, Alondra. I remember you were disturbed over our group's past rituals after Reardon left us. You knew it was wrong. Or are you blaming demons? Are you saying it's all their fault? I will never forgive you."

"I recall hearing forgiveness upon our last words," Alondra says with a solemn nod. "You thought I had left the world. You told me you forgave me. I hadn't left the world, but I felt every tear. But not even the High Priestess of the Hawthorne coven has any right to judge me."

"Who then? God?"

"I do not know," she says nodding slowly, almost thoughtful. Then she gestures behind her with an outstretched arm. "But I know them. Behold. These are the demons who reside on Earth. They move us, like puppeteers, into torment and rage. They are the shadows that hide behind every corner, every building, every tree. I could not see them in my life, but you can."

Alondra gazes down at my baby and smiles. Chandra's still crying like crazy. Can you blame her? It's so cold and dark under Alondra's shadow.

"*Are you teaching me again!*" I snap. Bryce has to grab Chandra so I don't drop her, I'm so pissed.

"Behold, Abaddon," she says calmly. "I am wicked. I am evil. Just as Liam can cast only black magic, your teacher can only teach evil. I refused to teach it when I was alive. Such black magic would have thwarted your attempts to cleanse me. But now, you summoned me. Here I am. Behold my final lesson."

I shake my head, preferring to look down at my baby. But it doesn't stop her from casting a shadow over us. Or from talking.

"I am A-L-O-N-D-R-A. *Revelare satanus.* Your adversary. The upside-down Sefirot. You cannot cast shadows in darkness, Cadence. Behind every light, darkness is. Cacodaemons. Ekimmu. Alu. Rakshasa. Satan. Evil exists and you cannot snuff it out, just as surely as you cannot cover the sun with the moon. Eclipse, perhaps? But even then, a ring of light remains and you won't see complete darkness. Dearest, if you truly understand what lies beneath you, then one day, maybe you might catch a glimpse of what lies above."

"I will never forgive you for what you did to my best friend!"

"Forgive yourself. I am dead. Show them now. Show them the shadows you abhor. Everyone around you, even those that seek to harm you, ones like me who stand before devils, seek peace. Show them evil. Amid shades, Melanie is pure. Enora is pure. The devils muddy everything." She signals to them, lurking behind her. "They soil us, Cadence, just as they degrade all the light in your world."

I hear their shrill, ear-piercing screams again. Everywhere among the wild grass of my backyard, like Enora's flock of ravens, hundreds of those horrible tall black figures are standing. And even without mouths, they scream the loudest shrill yell. It's almost as if they're objecting to everything Alondra is saying. Or...agreeing? In the back of my mind, I recall the pain in my stomach. I recall that knife. That is what their howling sounds like.

But, as my baby lies in my arms, I am calm. Everything is okay.

Except the wicked witch standing over me.

"Leave!" I say, still staring down at the baby. "Go away, Alondra! I don't want you near her! I'm done with you!"

"Goodbye, Cadence."

And she fades.

"Teach them my final lesson. Then teach Hawthorne all my lessons...teach the coven and your students everything I once taught you. Because...once, you loved Alondra."

Everywhere around our backyard, by tree trunks, by the logs of our bonfire, near chairs on our patio, and even inside the house, behind the large window in my bedroom, stand the dark, shadowy figures. I hear their shrill screams. I see their darkness.

So I remove my blindfold.

19

GNOSIS

"This is such a goddamn waste of time, Willow!" cries Enora, standing up at the table. "We've been here for over an hour. I told you guys séances are stupid. It's not going to stop your High Priestess from attacking us. If we can't reach Alondra or her ancestors, and get Katie free of her, I'm moving to plan B."

"Nothing's going to happen if you don't shut up," cries Mira.

Enora gestures around the room. "All I hear is static from that stupid ghost radio. And little Katie looks like she's fallen asleep."

"Are you all right, Cadence?" Bryce whispers, pushing my shoulder. "Katie? Wake up."

Yeah. Actually...I have never felt better. But I yawn... Maybe I was sleeping?

Everyone around the table is looking at me. Everyone except Mira and Enora. They're shouting at each other. And on the other side of the table, Aunt Jane and Liam look ready to join the fray.

Behind Mira and Kenosha, I see a few Ekimmu standing so

tall that they nearly touch the ceiling, just watching. I gaze down at the crystal ball I'm holding on my lap. It's emitting a lovely violet hue.

"I'm done!" Enora jumps up. She signals for Cordelia to join her. "That's it! Let's go. I should have known not to trust Raven. What an utter waste of time. She doesn't know shit. If the Hawthorne Witch can't figure out how to stop cursing us, Adder and the rest of my clan are going to have to take things into our own hands."

"Yeah, whatcha gonna do, bitch?" asks Maddie.

"You've already done enough to them!" snaps Aunt Jane.

"Sorry, Katie," Enora says. "Actually, I was beginning to like you. We're bound by dark magic, you know. But I can't care. My friends and I are more important than you."

"It's not me, Enora," I say.

"What?"

"It's not me," I say with a shrug. I turn to Jane and Liam and shake my head at them too. "It's not me, guys. And it's not Alondra, Abigail, or Escoba. Not even Melanie. It's no one."

"What, babe?" Maddie asks.

"I'm not casting any magic to harm her dreams, Maddie. I'm sure of it. Mira's séance worked. Alondra's gone."

Enora walks close, looking right over Kenosha's shoulder. Kenosha reels back. Then Enora snarls. "Who's cursing me then? Kindly tell the group. Tell me quick, or I'm gone. And when I'm gone, you and your friends are gone. Got me?"

But behind her is something so much more menacing. A tall, lanky faceless monster with shining white eyes is hovering over her. I laugh. It looks funny, in a sick, weird way. Here's a witch who prides herself on using fear to control people, and the dark, shadowy creature towering over her is far more terrifying than Enora could ever be.

"Have you finally lost your senses!" Enora snaps.

I point a finger at the creature behind her. Enora turns, but she doesn't see anything.

"Huh?" Enora asks. "What the hell do you mean, it's not you, Cadence? If it isn't you, come up with someone else that my Abaddon coven can take care of."

"It's him," I say, pointing a finger over her head.

"She has lost her marbles, master," Cordelia says.

"Who, Cadence?" asks Liam.

"You don't see him, Liam? Aunt Jane? Liam, you told me Kenosha had a demon possess you. There's one behind you, Liam. And one is standing right behind you, Enora. In fact, one or two stand behind each of us at the table. There are even a few of them by the door near Frida."

This finally freaks Enora out. She lurches back and searches all over the dark room. Everyone starts looking frantically behind their shoulders. Why can't they see them? There are as many of those dark, faceless giant spirits surrounding the table as there are people.

"You guys really don't see them?" I ask.

Bryce and Maddie shake their heads. Even Frida, who's still by the door, shakes her head.

"The EMF detector's been silent, Cadence," Raymond says. "We don't detect any ghosts now."

"They're not ghosts, Ray. They're demons. This is goetia. They're everywhere. This entire room is filled with devils. I remember reading about this in the...Berakhot. Alondra taught us this. Remember, Bryce? She said, according to ancient demonology, there lie thousands of demons to our left, and ten thousand on our right. You guys don't see them? The evil, Abaddon, is everywhere surrounding this table."

Kenosha furrows her brow and shakes her head.

I turn and see the transparent pitch-black clothes of the figure directly behind me. His creepy bright eyes stare down at me. I don't even need the crystal ball.

None of them move. They're just watching.

"Mazzikin," I explain. "You were right all along, Kenosha. You said I was haunted by a demon. I have been. We all have. These devils surround us. Believers pray, believing that their lord, God, is with them at all times, but few believe devils surround them too. Darkness comes with light. Demons preside over us all the time, so many evil spirits that they fill this room. I had never seen one before, until I had a vision during the séance. Alondra revealed them to me before she left me. Now I see them everywhere." I turn to Liam. "You told me you were possessed by an Ekimmu once, right?"

Liam nods. But then he shakes his head. "But I don't see anything, Cadence."

"*Because she's fucking mental!*" shouts Enora.

"Actually, I owe you the most, Enora," I say with a laugh. "Your blindfold spell taught me how to see in the dark. That's why Alondra wanted me to learn it. So I could finally show you. You know, guys, I learned that Escoba wasn't killed by Abigail. She killed herself. See, that's the lesson too. This darkness makes us hurt ourselves. It's not a person, it's a thing. This is evil. There's so much of this darkness surrounding us, guys, pulling us around like puppets. But each one of us is a bright light. Every one of us. Inside, we're not shadow. See, we are not evil deep inside, but the evil exists, surrounding us. Everywhere."

"What do you see, Katie!" Enora shouts. "Where? I've been sitting here for an hour and I don't see a damn thing!"

"Leave her alone!" cries Aunt Jane. "How could Alondra ever have taken you under her wing?"

"How could Falconsong have been your friend, old hag?" Enora shouts back.

And now Jane, Maddie, and Liam jump up. In another second, if I don't think of something, the whole room is going to turn into a brawl.

"We can see how good these old Hawthorne witches are, master," Cordelia says snidely. "Why not duel with a little magic? Perhaps do a little damage to this house again?"

"Splendid idea, Adder."

"It's okay, guys," I say. "Just sit down, Jane. Sit down, Maddie. Stop it, Enora. It's okay."

"Katie, ask Adder what I've been preparing," cries Enora. "We have everything—"

"Whatever you're planning," Jane says, "we'll shield her. That's why Liam and I are here. To protect Cadence from you!"

"Or cast something far worse," Liam adds.

"Oh, let's see, warlock," Enora says. "I'd love to see what you got. And you too, green witch. Alondra told me of your powers. I think I can match it. But for now, Adder, let's leave. This is hardly fair. Only you and I against two old geezers and little Katie's entire coven on her hallowed ground. Anyway—" She gazes around the dark room. "Katie will go see a shrink and you and I can take care of this circle later."

"Enora," I say quietly. I'm the only one still sitting.

She spins around.

"Your nightmares will end after we save Melanie. This curse is not from me, you, or her. Nor is it Alondra. It's not from any *person*. It's from the grounds. It's an energy, like a witch's hallowed grounds. But we need to help each other in order to fight it. Fighting each other is not going to stop it, it's going to grow it. The evil has soiled Melanie's life, and all her suffering is our fault."

"*F-u-c-k you*," Enora drawls, raising an eyebrow. "Muddy-bitch has messed with us time and time again. Maybe she finally messed with your brain."

"Remove your blindfold, Raven," Alondra says.

It's not from my lips, it's coming from somewhere in the room. It freaks everybody out. Enora laughs nervously. But hearing Alondra makes her and Cordelia suddenly not want to leave. Maybe she's finally thinking the séance wasn't a failure? And then, the answer comes to me. I don't know how, or why, but it just does. I know exactly what to do.

With my right hand, I lift my violet orb from the table and hold it aloft, high above my head. There's a flash of brilliant violet light. It's such a bright purple light that I have to turn and squint. Then I hear the shattering of the glass as the quartz explodes into shards of crystal in my palm. All that's left in my right hand is a small flickering flame with the gem's dust and a few small shards of crystal. Then I shake the flames from my hand. It leaves a violet glow about the room.

I hear gasps. But it's not a reaction to my exploding orb.

Standing behind everyone around the table, now illuminated by the bright violet glow, are faceless demons. But now they're not visible just to me, but everyone at the table sees them.

Enora and Cordelia fall on the ground behind Kenosha. They're extending their arms, trying to keep the monsters away. Josie and Beth scream. Then Maddie and Frida cry out. But the demons, the Ekimmu, don't stir. They never move. They're just here. Like watchers. That's what angels and demons were once called, right? Watchers? They watch us, immobile. They don't have to move—they control us anyway.

"Everyone, hold hands," I say.

Everyone around the table except Enora and Cordelia obey me. It's as if we're restarting the séance, only I'm officiating now.

"Inside we shine light," I say to everyone around me with a nod. "Outside is evil. Not you. Or you. Our hands burn like fire. The fire of our bodies shelters us from the cold. The demons are cold. *Lux alba et tenebris.* See what surrounds you."

"*My god, they're everywhere!*" Enora cries.

Enora sounding so scared is terrifying.

But, slowly, the demons fade.

All becomes silent. Nobody says a word. I'm reminded of the time Enora showed my coven a gateway to hell. That was an illusion, but my whole coven was in shock. That is how everyone is now. But now, oddly, the witches who seem to be in the most shock are Enora and Cordelia.

Kenosha's gazing down at the table, almost pensively, nodding. So are Jane and Liam. Poor Maddie is shaking in my brother's arms. Bryce's body is shaking too. Frida and the ghost hunters have fled the room.

"I need everyone's help," I say quietly, slowly letting go of Bryce's and Maddie's hands. "I need you, Willow. You too, Jane, and you, Liam. I need you, Enora. I need every witch here. Can you guys go with me to Geneva Forest? Witches cursed Melanie. We made her into mud. It's our fault. Once we rescue her, I believe Hawthorne will finally be at peace. So will your coven, Enora."

But everyone is still in far too much shock to respond.

I let go of Bryce's and Maddie's shaking hands. And Enora and Cordelia slowly rise.

The violet light in the room fades. It is replaced by all the flickering yellow candles. I think they can't see the Ekimmu anymore. I still see them. All it takes is a little concentration, and the dark beasts tower behind everyone again.

"Cadence, that was pure quartz!" snaps Kenosha. Her breaking the silence causes me to jump. "Do you have any idea how valuable that crystal ball was?"

But she's not really mad. She has a huge grimace on her face. I think that for her my magic show, not the orb breaking but my revelation, was worth all the money and sentimental value in the world.

"Guess we're going back to Alabama, guys," quips Mira.

Bryce vehemently shakes his head. I quickly grab his hand and squeeze it tightly.

"I need you, babe," I whisper in his ear. "Sorry."

Enora and Cordelia stand up. And we all finally found our ghosts from Mira's séance. My archenemies' faces are ashen white.

"I need you there too, Enora."

20

SANDWICHES

I'M EATING A DELICIOUS PHILLY CHEESESTEAK AT THE LOCAL
sandwich shop not far from Maddie's house. It's the afternoon
after our extremely weird séance experience. Frida and Maddie
are across from me in a hard plastic yellow booth. Frida's eating
a turkey sandwich, and Maddie's got a Monte Carlo. I keep
taking only a few bites. We're all still freaked out over my weird
cathartic shit yesterday.

The window is farther down a narrow hall in the restaurant,
so it's a little dark this far inside the shop. This is a shame
because it's a nice day outside. I would have loved to sit by the
window, but all the booths are at this end of the restaurant.
They really should put tables and chairs outside.

The sandwich parlor has been here for years. It used to be
one of our favorite stops during the summers I stayed at
Maddie's house. Like I said, the decor sucks, but the sand-
wiches are totally dope.

"Thanks for coming, guys," I say, sucking my soda with a
straw.

"What did you want to talk about, Katie?" Frida asks. Then

she looks around the restaurant and chuckles. "Are those demons still around us?"

"Yeah."

Maddie and Frida lose their smiles.

"We need to reschedule the wedding."

There. Done. I might as well just get it right out in the open.

Frida nods contemplatively. Madison doesn't. She looks real pissed.

"Cadence, the catering, decorations, and flower arrangements are all set for Sunday," Maddie says. "I've got a special photographer coming in from Atlanta, all the dresses are on loan, and the church date was nearly impossible to arrange. You know, Hawthorne Church is the only church in town. And your dad has insisted on being married in a church. So, no. Not to mention that all our special guests—" She hugs Frida. "Like this one, won't be here later. As stressful as your life is—and I know it's been horrible lately, babe—I'm Mom's wedding planner, and we have to get our parents married this weekend."

"Greg and I can come back another time," Frida says.

"Until I figure out how to keep these things at bay—"

"What things?" Maddie snaps. "Cadence, even Liam didn't get it. Who are we fighting? Every one of us saw the devils you manifested. It sure shut up Enora and Cordelia, and, yeah, it completely freaked us out, but none of us totally gets what your show meant. So there are demons everywhere? What are we going to do about it? You told us they've been here since before we came to Hawthorne. Then you confused the hell out of Mom when you said those Ekimmus are in every town, every city, in every part of the world, around every corner. So who the hell are we fighting?"

"They were terrible," Frida says.

"They sure fucking were, Freeds," Maddie says with a nod. "But what of it? If the demons have been here since before we came to Hawthorne, why delay the wedding? We didn't delay the rehearsal, and it still went fine. Enora's not going to crash into your car. She's more afraid of you than ever. And why would Melanie dare curse you, now that you're this new badass witch?"

"That's where you're wrong, Maddie," I say. "Melanie could hurt your mom and my dad if we don't talk to her now. Especially in their wedding ceremony. So we need to go down to Alabama right away. It's the *grounds* in Alabama that destroyed Melanie. I told you guys, it's the grounds in Alabama, just like the land a haunted house stands on, that's causing Melanie's evil. Alondra and Kenosha worsened the curse, all the witches did, but Kenosha thinks the grounds were cursed even before. I know that the only way to save Melanie is to get her away from there. She suffers every day, Maddie. She needs to leave that place...it's...it's going to be almost impossible to convince her, but if I had known before, I would have taken her home before. The energy there is so bad. And if we don't help Melanie, yes, Maddie, she's apt to hurt us again."

"But then Melanie's the problem, Katie," Frida says gently.

"I think part of the reason Alondra kept popping up," I say, shaking my head, "is Alondra believed she, no, *we*, as Hawthorne witches, ruined Melanie's life. She should have been helped out of that wretched place long ago. Alondra failed her. It's my job to help her now."

"Cadence," Maddie says, lifting a brow and opening her eyes wide, "so what's your plan? You're going to open the door of Bryce's BMW and put this crouching, filthy, smelly beast in his car, then drive her back home with you?"

I laugh because Maddie sounds ridiculous. But then I nod.

Maddie throws her hair back and plops back in her booth.

She stares at the wall.

"Katie didn't show me anything in that room I didn't already know was there, Maddie," Frida says. "That's why I left. You just showed us what I was afraid of all along, guys. We have no right seeing it. It is evil. Satan. It's darkness that shadows the light of our lord, God, Jesus Christ."

"Frida, as always, I don't want to see them, okay," I say. "I didn't ask for this dark magic, just like I didn't ask for any magic. But if I can help people, is it bad, guys? Alondra told me in my vision that by seeing evil, I might be able to do some good. And now, I think I might be able to use it to help get Melanie out."

"We didn't need to see them." Frida's head is in her hands. "Nobody does. We just have to have faith, Cadence. That's all we need. Faith."

And then Frida starts crying. Maddie turns and rubs her back.

"Oh, Frida," Maddie says. "It's okay."

"Maddie," she says in a broken voice, shaking her head, "Katie has to find peace. That's all I want. For their baby. I love Aunt Jane and her dad's so nice, but if Katie's sure she needs to do this to find peace, then Maddie, we have to let—"

"*No!*" Maddie snaps. "No! No fucking way I'm going back there, Frida! This will be the—" She looks up for a moment, in thought, and sighs while counting on her fingers. "What, like fiftieth time you're visiting that filth, Cadence? She's not even a person."

"The last time," I say. "The last time, Madison. And, yeah, I'm planning on bringing her back home with me."

"What if she doesn't want to go?" Frida looks up, wiping her eyes.

"Maddie," I say.

I look deeply into her eyes, and my bestie already knows what I'm going to say. I'm a firm believer now that she's psychic. It's not only our love for each other, it's her magic power. I might see demons, but she can read my mind.

I tell her anyway.

"Maddie, I'm not going to be able to go to Alabama and

make it back to the wedding in time if you don't reschedule. If you can't reschedule, then...I'm going to have to miss the wedding. I'm sorry, but I don't see any other choice. It's too dangerous."

"*Bitch*," Maddie mutters, turning from me to face the wall. "You never wanted to go."

"Yeah, well, Frida's right, I have to fix Hawthorne for my family. *Our* family. My family includes your mom now. I love your mom so much, Maddie, whether she becomes *my* mom or not. But I have to help Melanie. I just have to. And it has to be done now, or I don't even want to know what could happen during Dad's wedding. Or Hawthorne. Or, god, even on Halloween. As hard as this is—"

"Cadence, why can't you go after the weekend!" Maddie snaps. "I mean, what the fuck? What happened in that trance of yours, anyway? Did you achieve some amazing spiritual awakening? Hallelujah, Cadence, you're Hawthorne's new prophet! Now what about our *mom and dad!*"

"No awakening, Maddie," I say with a sigh. "I just saw what's in front of my eyes."

"*If there are thousands of demons everywhere, what does it matter if you get rid of a handful of them!*" Maddie cries. "*And why do you have to do it on Mom's wedding day!*"

"*Because we're all in danger from Melanie if I don't, Maddie! Come on. Enora's accusing me! She's accusing me. I now know it's not me. If it isn't me, who do you think is doing this to her?*"

And now I'm staring at the wall too.

"Don't do this," I say. "Please. I can...help her. If I do that, something Alondra could never do, Alondra can rest in peace. Hawthorne can be at peace. And I can ensure the wedding is peaceful."

"Why didn't Alondra fucking do this when she was alive! Huh? Bring out her ghost right now so I can slug her!"

We laugh.

"Maybe she tried?" I ask. "But how would Alondra help a girl that she, herself, cursed? I never cursed her. That's probably why only I can help her. I can get her out of that hell. I have to try. I just know I have to try. It will finally free us. And maybe free Alondra—not just from me, but maybe help her go in peace to the Summerland. I know it can make things right."

"By skipping out on your dad and Mom's wedding!"

"Maddie!" Frida says vehemently, shaking her head. "No. She says she has to."

"Bryce is right," Maddie says. "You're so fucking stubborn, Cadence! The minute you have something in your head, it's absolutely impossible to change it."

"Her element is Earth," Frida says with a shrug.

"It sure is, Freeds. Why the hell are you on her side?" Maddie asks.

"I'm not. I...I just think Katie's gone through so much. If she thinks this can solve it, we need to let her try. We need to help her, Maddie. You told me to be there for her when she was cursed."

"I'm not asking you guys to cancel the wedding," I say. "I think...you probably *should* cancel the ceremony, to be safe, but I can't ask you to do that."

Maddie looks down at her cellphone, shaking her head. Then, with her other hand, she presents her middle finger.

"Well, Katie-bitch, sorry, but no. We already spoke about the risks and agreed to still plan the wedding for tomorrow. Right now it's twelve-thirty. It takes at least three hours to drive through the forest to that fucking horror show. That means you can bring that monster home by late tonight or early tomorrow and still make it to your dad's wedding. But, nope, there's no fucking way I am rescheduling everything now."

"I don't know if I'll make it," I say. "But...I get it."

"My mom and your dad will wait at Hawthorne Church," Maddie says with a very fake grin, grabbing her purse. Frida stands up to let her out of the booth. "Better be there, or there'll be hell to pay, not just from muddy-bitch or demons. From me, my mom, and your dad. Got me?"

I nod.

"Oh, and, good luck convincing your husband. You don't have a car after Enora crashed it, remember?"

She rushes down the hallway in a total huff. I look at Frida across the table. Then I bite into my sandwich.

Frida frowns.

"Can you drive me home, Frida?"

"Sure, Katie."

"I think she forgot she drove me here."

"I'm not so sure she forgot."

21

MY PLAN

Bryce hasn't been talking to me. I get it. Funny thing is, we're not fighting. I think he's just freaked out. Something about my spectacle at the Billington House told him to expect something weird this week. He hasn't even said a word about missing the wedding. Really, he hasn't said a thing at all (but I heard him throwing things around in our bedroom closet while he was getting dressed, preparing to drive me back to Geneva Forest).

As we slowly pass over that ridiculous, terrifying rickety old narrow bridge once more, I try again.

"Your last lecture about Dracula was cool, babe. I really loved it."

I touch his arm. He just nods.

Then he's back to scanning the forest. I am too. But despite the butterflies roaming in my stomach, the forest is pretty. It always is. Geneva Forest reminds me a little of Hawthorne, you know, with all the tall, thin trees surrounding woodland pools and wild grass. It's a really lovely wilderness.

"Not only was the Vlad the Impaler history stuff cool, Bryce, but you made me want to vacation there and visit Transylvania. I totally want to go see Bran Castle now."

"Don't tell me we're going there next!" he snaps.

That makes us laugh. I grab his hand.

"You think I'm getting big?"

"No, Katie," he says, rubbing my belly.

But then he's back to scoping out the forest. I'm looking for eyes watching us in the trees. You know, Melanie's eyes, white eyes in the midst of the muddiest face, a filthy beast crouched down behind bushes. It kind of feels like I'm searching for Sasquatch. Somehow, I feel like she watches me, like Enora, out there. And, with all these shadowy trees, you can kind of feel her staring at us.

The sky is clear with only a few wisps of white clouds around the bright yellow sun. Rays of yellow light flicker through all the passing leaves. Some of the trees are red and orange with fall colors, but most are green. I've caught a few woodpeckers. Bryce and I even saw a small fox cross the road. You'd think we've been here enough times that we wouldn't have any trouble finding Mud, but, actually, Bryce has to be careful where he drives. The road deeper in the forest is unmarked, without any signs that will lead us to her lair.

"Liar," I blurt. I shake my head hard, trying to think of something else. Then I lean back in my seat, stretching out my arms. "I'm getting bigger. So? It's expected."

"You look beautiful, babe."

"But bigger."

"Sure. Okay."

"Hey...Bryce, how come you haven't asked me what the plan is when we see the Samhain Witch?"

"Because I don't want to know."

And he doesn't. He stops talking.

Now we're winding up that woodsy, bumpy hill where he has to drive more slowly over rocks and ditches.

I glance at my side mirror. I'm surprised to see headlights behind us, in the distance, down a grassy, green ravine. It's not dark yet, but some drivers put their headlights on for safety when driving these windy turns. It looks like there are headlights behind us. That's weird. I was napping most of the way, so I didn't notice anyone behind us.

And then, at the crest of the hillside, I can't believe my eyes. In the center of the forest, in Melanie's large grassy glade, there must be twenty cars parked. The decrepit shack, which was just an illusion, has been replaced by cars parked along the grassy glade.

"What's going on, Bryce?"

"You told Maddie." He shuts the engine off and smirks. "Well, we're here. So what's the plan?"

A car parks behind us. It's Mira's black van again. Well, I knew *she* would be here. But I hardly expected to see Maddie standing by her mom. My brother is with her, and Frida, Kenosha, and Liam, all beside Aunt Jane's blue jeep. Everyone but Frida is wearing a cloak. Aunt Jane and Kenosha are wearing forest-green robes. But, aside from this group having transported nearly all of Hawthorne to Alabama, I'm amazed to see Maddie. I mean, *Madison*, can you believe it? Maddie swore to never come here again after last Halloween. Not to mention, well, you remember our row over lunch.

"You don't mind if your car gets dirty, do you, Bryce?"

"Huh?" He just looks at me funny. "What do you mean?"

Never mind.

In the far distance to my left, closer to the trees, I see about ten people wearing scarlet robes. This must be Enora's Abaddon coven. Some have hoods over their heads; others are smoking cigarettes, folding their arms, and acting cool. Two witches, most distinctively, are wearing shades and sitting on the hood of a paint-chipped gray SUV, as if they're preparing for a drive-in movie. Leaning against that car with folded arms, is that horrible witch Cordelia. The leader of the delinquents, Enora, is walking over to us.

"Maddie brought the whole goddamn town," I say.

"She's a good friend, Cadence," Bryce says with a rueful grin and nod. Then he kisses my cheek. He adds in a whisper, "Now, go out there and do whatever the hell you have to do so you, me, and our little girl never have to come back here ever again. Okay?"

"Yeah. Sure, babe."

I face him and gently touch my lips to his. He leans closer, running his hands through my long hair. And then we smooch. And it's...so nice.

"I really love you, Bryce."

"I don't want to be here." He looks around at the surrounding forest. But then he turns back. So I kiss his lips some more.

"*Cut this shit out!*" shouts Enora, banging on my passenger window. We lurch back. "*Fuck! Let's get on with this!*"

I open my door—a little hard—trying to hit her. Then Bryce and I get out and put on our black cloaks.

I completely ignore Enora, rushing over to my friends and landing in Maddie's arms.

"The wedding," I cry. "What the hell are you doing when there's a wedding?"

"No one's having a wedding without you, Cadence," Maddie says with a chuckle, hugging me tightly.

"And why don't you hate me?"

"Yeah, I hate you."

"They called it off, Katie," Frida says with a wave and a grin. "We love you too much." But then she looks at the grassy field. Her expression changes to fear. "This is that horrible place?"

"Yep," Maddie says, looking scared too. "Muddy-bitch's lair."

"None of us want to be here," Liam says, walking over. "So do whatever you have to do for Allie's spirit and Hawthorne, and then let's never come back here again." Hmm...I don't have any arguments with him this time.

"Ah, Katie's having a reunion?" asks Enora behind my back. "How sweet."

"I don't think you and Kenosha should be here, Liam," I say, ignoring Enora again. "That witch hates you more than anyone."

"We're here under your lead," says Kenosha solemnly, shaking her head. "What are you planning to do to finally cleanse these grounds, Windstorm?"

Kenosha's bald, decked out in gold necklaces and earrings, and looks totally witchy. She looks excited, just like in the séance after I blew up her crystal ball. It reminds me of Mira. I guess Kenosha came to Hawthorne not for me, but for their "chosen one." I hardly feel chosen just because I can see demons, though.

"We either get Melanie out or, somehow, I make the demons haunting her leave," I say to everyone. "But...I don't think I can get rid of the demons."

"Can you still see them?" Kenosha asks.

I survey the field. Yes. Do you see them? The dark shadows, the Ekimmu, are everywhere—tall, lanky, immobile black spirits shadowed in darkness. They're terrifying. But they never move. They're just wraith-like creatures, reminding me of black see-through shrouds. The only thing that flutters, like flags, is their bodies. They fold and contort in the wind but are otherwise completely motionless. I wish I didn't see them. All these other witches are lucky. But, the funny thing is, I think Kenosha would give anything in the world to see them too.

More of the witches from my coven rush over. Josie, Debra, and Abella hug me. Then I'm surprised to see young Cat, the ghost hunter. I should have known she and her dad, Raymond, would come. And standing by me are the newbies, Nancy and Beth. Then comes Mira, waving. She's with Courtney. I mean everyone, everybody from Hawthorne, is here. It makes me feel kinda sad. They were supposed to be at Dad's wedding. And, of all people, Dad's missing.

"Well, Cadence," Enora says, with total bitchy smugness, "what are those demons saying to you? Huh? Do they want to nudge muddy-bitch out of hiding? Or would you like me to summon my birds again?"

"Did you bring Aamon's wand?"

"Yes."

"That'll do."

Then I turn to the group.

Wow, this isn't like a Sabbath, it's like a lecture. I actually feel bashful before so many people. And a couple more cars are still arriving. I catch Gilda's white SUV. I wave. Shit, all the witches of my coven, even the newbies, are here. Not to mention everyone from Enora's coven in Atlanta.

"Guys," I say loudly, "I love it that all of you came to support me, but—"

"They came for the Hawthorne Witch," Kenosha says very sternly. "All these witches, Windstorm, stand under your lead."

"Well, I love it…you're so sweet, but you guys don't get it. I have to go alone. Melanie is shy, even shyer than I am. If all of us walk into the field, I don't think she'll show herself. And, Liam, Kenosha, you two have to stay back. She hates you more than anybody."

"I'm not keeping back," Enora says. "'Fraid Samhain's got some explaining to do."

"I was counting on that. You, Bryce, Maddie, and I will go. The rest of you need to stay back."

"I'm going, Cadence?" Maddie asks, creeped out as hell. Of all people, she doesn't want to move another step.

"Yes, Maddie. You…you don't have to go, but you came here

for me, right? I need your love. We're besties. And I need you to show that to Melanie. You and Bryce. I need you guys beside me." Then I turn to Enora's pretty face. Why was this horrible person blessed with the prettiest face? "And even you. You three are my balance. My lux alba et tenebris."

"So, I'm tenebris?" asks Enora with a laugh. "Fine, Cadence."

"Yeah. Like in our ceremony, both alba et tenebris. Melanie has to see that balance. I don't know why, I just know it, like I knew I had to show you all Kenosha's crystal ball. I just feel it, you know."

"Whatever, Windstorm," Enora says. Then she peers at the glade. Even she seems apprehensive. "Let's just get this over with."

I follow her gaze. I will myself to not see those dark shadows, because I don't want to see them. So they fade. Even one that was standing behind Enora disappears. They all disappear by my will, thank God.

"Cadence!"

I jump like a hundred feet and then spin around. It's Tammy taking me into her arms.

"Hi, Tamms!"

"Hey, Katie," says Gilda, behind her, with a wave. She hugs me too. And her friends Natasha and Mandy behind them.

"We all hitched a ride with Gilda from Savannah," Tammy says. "We're so worried." She looks curiously out at the field. "This is it? It doesn't look scary, guys. It just looks like a dead, grassy field. This is that terrible place you keep talking about?"

"Uh, yeah, Tamms," says Maddie. Then she points down at her feet. "Look down. See how nice and flat the grass is here? We're standing in a space where we went exploring last Halloween, only we were *inside* a house. The house completely disappeared."

"Don't even talk about it, Maddie," says Frida. "It's so terrible."

"You have the whole coven here, Cadence." Tammy has turned serious, like Kenosha. "All the new witches and all us ole veterans under Alondra. So? What do you need us to do to help you finally take care of this monster for good?"

"Everyone stay here and wait for me."

Tammy doesn't mind. Neither does Frida. Neither do so many other witches. But Kenosha, Liam, and Aunt Jane don't look so sure.

"Cadence, I helped create this evil," Kenosha objects. "You should let me try to cleanse the grounds with you. I should speak to her too."

"No, Kenosha." I shake my head. "You told me once she'd kill you if she saw you. You have to stay back."

"Will you and I ever stop fighting?"

"No." But I laugh.

Kenosha nods. Then she turns to Enora. That wipes the smile from Kenosha's face. "No tricks, Panthera. The council will be dealing with you and—" She glances over at the sea of red robes fifty yards away. "The rest of your villains when this is over. Back to jail you're going. A jail without windows."

"Love and kisses to you too, Willow," Enora says. "Shall we, Katie?"

The two of us walk farther out into the wild grass. Bryce is holding *Broomstick* in one hand and my hand in the other. I cock my head back, and everyone is just standing there and watching us.

Maddie's trailing far behind us. I gesture for her to hurry up. She shakes her head.

"So you really see evil spirits now?" Enora asks me. "A little touch of my magic and, poof, you're the world's expert necromancer?"

"I guess."

"Well, you realize, of course, Cadence," Enora infernally continues, "that just because the Samhain Witch is driven by these demons, that does not mean she wasn't responsible. I must admit, I'm impressed with your ploy. It's very clever to remove responsibility from the true offender to protect her from me. What a brilliant way of making us all *friends*. But you've given away too much. Whether the Ekimmus possess muddy-bitch or whether the spells were actually from you, whoever spell casts against my Abaddon coven and me is going to pay."

"We already know that, Enora," says Bryce.

"And why the hell is a stupid, weak man joining us?"

"He's my husband and I love him. He's also Hawthorne's High Priest."

"Yeah...but why is a *man* with us?"

"Melanie needs to see him. And I need him by my side."

And he holds my hand tighter.

"You're here for the wand, Enora," I say. "If you double cross me, I will turn the demons presiding over these grounds on you. And this land has more demons than I've ever seen."

That disturbs her and I have to hide a grin. You know, I think she and her henchwoman, Cordelia, were more disturbed than anyone else by my vision in the Billington House.

"Can you guys slow down," Maddie says from behind, out of breath. "Jeesh. What's wrong with you! Is there some rush to see that horrible monster again?"

Enora just rolls her eyes.

Then a cloud darkens the grass before our path, and soon it's dark everywhere. That disturbs us. We're not sure if it's nature or Melanie. But we keep walking. My plan is simple. I'm trying to get as far away as I can so that I can no longer hear or see my friends' faces. I don't want them hurt, and I don't want to intimidate Melanie.

We slow down, hearing whispers among the nearby trees.

It's faint, like wind among the leaves, but I hear it. So does Enora. So do Bryce and Maddie. We turn to the forest, scanning the trees.

And then I stop.

"This is as good a place as any."

"For what?" Bryce asks.

"To knock on her door."

"Ah, the great necromancer permits us to halt," Enora quips.

"Take out your wand and find her, Enora." But I quickly raise a hand. "*Find her,* don't strike her. Remember my warning."

Enora squints as she searches the trees on both sides of us. She puts a finger to her cheek. "My birds could sure help." But then she pulls out her thin black wand. "I will permit you to lead for the time being, until we find muddy-bitch, Katie. But when she's found, you and your friends are on your own. Remember the parley? Well, consider this a truce. None of us are friends."

"I know, Enora. Just find her."

"Sure thing."

She closes her eyes, takes the black book with an upside-down pentagram from under her arm, and holds it close to her chest.

"*Revelare,*" Enora says. "*Revelare.* Come forth and manifest Mud. Upon the change of seasons. From Mabon to Samhain, Ostara to Beltane. Upon Samhain again, and again, on the wheel of bledani, manifest muddy-bitch. *Samhain. Samhain.* Show her to me. Reveal. *Revelare. Revelare.* Samhain Witch."

Enora points the thin black stick all around her. It shakes in some directions. But then...nothing. Even the whispers disappear.

She swings the wand in the other direction, slashing it like a sword. And then she turns to face the large grassy field. Nothing...

She turns to me, throws her hands up, and shrugs.

"We need my birds."

"Are you trying?"

"Of course I'm trying! What do you think? I haven't used Aamon's wand since we trapped her last time."

"Try again."

She squints her eyes, suddenly looking dangerous. "Are you ordering me, Cadence?"

"Just, please try again, Enora."

She smiles a sly grin.

She turns her back on us again and holds her black book aloft with her wand. She taps the wand on her black book, as if she's a conductor in an orchestra. She lowers her head, closes her eyes, and sighs, and she says again, *"Revelare. Revalare. Manifesta Samhain. Manifesta. Fucking manifesta now!"*

But...nothing.

"Maybe I should try?" Maddie asks sarcastically.

"What?" Enora asks with her eyes still closed. She whirls back on Maddie. "Shut up! Why the hell are you even here, Blackbird? I'm trying—"

"Hand it to Bryce," I say.

"What?"

"It's the wand of a magus, right?" I repeat. "Hand the wand to Bryce, Enora."

"Why am I even fucking listening to you!" Enora shouts. She gets right up to my face. "How dare you order me around. I'm telling you, the way to do this is to survey the grass with my ravens."

"If you summon birds, Melanie will think we're fighting."

"Who says we aren't?"

Enora is standing close, too close.

"She needs our help, Enora," I reply, shaking my head.

"She's confused. She needs us to help her. We don't need to hurt her."

Bryce pushes Enora from me. That pisses Enora off more than ever. I hear Enora's minions behind us shouting in the distance.

"Stop it, Bryce," I say. "I'm fine."

"Don't touch her!" Bryce snaps, wagging a finger. "Back away from Cadence, Enora."

"I should have finished you when I had you bound in Gus's house," Enora snaps. "You've always been in the way of our witchcraft, first Alondra's, now your wife's."

"Cut it out, guys," says Maddie. "Stop fighting!"

A great many spirits surround us. The Ekimmu. There must be twenty behind Enora. Her anger seems to be evoking more and more.

Goety. Goety. Goety.

"Enora, you're bringing them here!"

"You don't lead me, Katie, 'kay? You don't order me around. Nobody orders me around. Even *Allie* knew that. Got me?"

She points a finger into my chest. Bryce bats her hand off.

"Bryce, stop!"

"You bitch!" Maddie shouts at Enora. "No one's ordering you. We're here for the same thing."

There's more shouting from the witches back by the cars.

"One more touch, even a brush of my robe," Enora warns Bryce, "and I'll light your hand on fire, just like Katie did to me."

"I'm not the one who keeps getting in her face," Bryce snaps.

"It's all right, Bryce, forget it," I say, putting my hands up in front of everyone. "Come on, guys. Just stop fighting."

"Why is she even here, Cadence!" shouts Maddie. "Why would you bring her here? Is she cursing you again?"

"I told you. I need her beside us, Maddie."

"Well, I don't need you," Enora says. Then she shouts in my face, "*Cadere!*"

I'm struck by a force of wind. But I don't fall...until she thrusts her black wand before my eyes. A powerful gust of wind throws me on the grass. I hear laughter from the crowd. Then shouting.

"You bitch!" cries Maddie.

But Maddie doesn't charge her, Bryce does. Hard. Enora's thrown to the ground. That does it for the spectators. Black- and red-robed witches run toward us, but, just like two years ago in the grassy field under our library, they don't get far before they start fighting each other—not with magic, but with fists.

Bryce wrestles Enora. Then Maddie kicks Enora's head viciously, and Enora closes her eyes.

"Maddie!" I shout, getting up on my knees. "What are you guys doing! What are all of you doing!"

"She shouldn't have come here!" shouts Maddie.

"*Cadere,*" Enora seethes quietly through her teeth. Maddie and Bryce are thrown from her. Then Enora stands. "I should have killed you too when you betrayed my coven, Blackbird."

Bryce tackles Enora again. And this time, he slugs her in the face.

"*Stop fighting!*" I shout. "*What are you doing!*" I have to pull Bryce off Enora, preventing another blow. Then I point back at the melee behind us. "Stop them, Enora!"

"What the hell did you expect, stupid?" Enora shouts. "Nobody, including me, has been sleeping! You want to *save* Melanie? I'd do anything to kill you both!"

"I hate her!" cries Maddie, on her knees, in tears. "I hate her so much, Cadence,"

"Well, I'm not your *friend!*" Enora says, shoving me to the ground again.

"*Grab the wand, Bryce!*" I cry.

The shadows are everywhere. So many cover the fields they darken the sky. There are like a hundred demons covering the glade. Some of them are hovering over me now, their black bodies flapping or fluttering in the wind.

"*Goetia*," I bark, looking up. "*Goetia! Goetia!*"

Enora freezes with her black wand still held aloft. Then I turn to the commotion behind us. "*Goetia! Goetia!*"

The demons fly over the field, like Enora's ravens once did, and swoop over the onlookers. Each scarlet-robed witch freezes as it is touched by a shade, but my friends in black robes are spared. The demons seem to obey my power now.

I spin around to Bryce.

"Wave Enora's wand around, Bryce, and find Melanie. Summon her. We have to end this."

Bryce nods but he has that look of bewilderment I'm so familiar with when casting an unfamiliar spell. Holding the thin black wand aloft, he says hesitantly, "*Revelare. Revelare. Samhain Witch. Come forth. Revelare.*"

The wand seems to pull his hand toward the trees to our left.

A figure crouched over in the woods moves slowly toward us under the shade of branches and leaves. If I hadn't seen the Samhain Witch before, I'd have thought this was an animal. But when she breaks from the forest canopy, I see her filth. A mud-coated woman with sagging breasts and filthy underwear slowly approaches us. A black serpent is slithering around her filthy neck. And those eyes, so white and creepy, amid all the leaves and dark muck. When she's about thirty yards from me, she stops.

Enora is still immobile, facing the other direction. Her goons aren't moving either. The violence behind us is over.

Melanie doesn't come any closer. She just stands there.

"Melanie, I came here to help you."

"Help me?" she croaks. Then she points at Enora. "Or help her? Is she my friend?"

"Sure, Melanie. We're all your friends."

"And you?" she asks, shuffling toward Maddie. She comes close enough for Maddie to back up, wrinkling her nose in revulsion. "And you?" she asks with a bigger smile, approaching Bryce. "What a handsome man Cassie-Hasshorn brings to me."

"Bryce," he says, touching his chest.

"*Bryce?*" Melanie says with a nod and a disgusting grin. "Bryce. A pleasure to meet you." She turns to me and points to the shadows circling in the sky. "Do you see *my* friends now, Cassie?"

"Yes."

"How can you possibly help me?"

"I want you to leave this place."

"But this is my home, witch," she says, shaking her head. "I didn't send for them. You witches—*tell them to stay back!*"

I lurch back. Melanie has been speaking so softly and carefully, her shout is jarring. She points at the elder witches—Liam, Aunt Jane, and Kenosha—walking across the grass toward me.

"Stay back, guys," I holler. "Stay back by the cars."

Melanie's hideous gray cracked lips part in a smile.

"You bring more people than ever," Melanie says. "I don't think we've ever had so many visitors, Momma. Why? Are you here to visit as a *friend*?" Then she bursts into laughter. "Ain't that what that witch Eee-noora said? She called you her friend. She's very funny."

"I'm here to help you."

"*Liar!*" she croaks. She shuffles right up to my face and then opens her creepy eyes wide. "All I ask is truth, all I ask is for nice nice Cassie-Cassie to not lie to Melanie. I don't like lies, don't lie to me, Cassie. You are not here to help me, you...are... here for me to help you. Is that not right? Tell the truth. You came because your poor friend—*Eeenoora*—has trouble sleeping. That poor evil witch can't close her eyes without seeing something scary. And her friends can't sleep either. Yes?"

"Yes."

"Do you know why?"

"Because of the shadows."

"No! No! No! It is not because of the dear shadows that blanket my lovely field. It is because of me. I bring them nightmares. She is a bad, bad witch, Cassie. She had you come here and try to kill me, if you don't remember. I remember. Are you stupid?"

"But you have to stop attacking her."

"Why? You helped her. Yes, I remember, Momma. She helped us, didn't she. Cassie is my friend. She healed me. Tell the Samhain Witch what present she may offer you so you can finally get the fuck out of her house?"

Then she laughs.

"I just ask for peace. Peace in Hawthorne and for my friends. If you don't leave with me, at least stop haunting our sleep."

"Peace lies under the ground when you die. Peace is a wildflower lying alone atop a lovely mahogany coffin by a tombstone. Peace is the rancid honey of dead carrion bees lying on a field of ash or tarmac wound up in fabric wraps. Alondra wants peace. She found it. Kenosha wants peace. She doesn't have it. Liam wants peace. He lives in the hell where he belongs. Everyone wants peace. Including my dear sister Winona. But no one asks little ole me what I want."

"What do you want?" asks Bryce.

"Shush, Bryce," I say. "No."

Melanie shuffles quickly to Bryce. Her eyes open wide again.

"Such a handsome man. So tall and strong. Brave? Tell me... *Bryce*, is your wife...*pregnant?*" Then, as she continues to stare at his face, her fingers, with long misshapen filthy fingernails, glide over my stomach. "Going to have a nice cute, cuddly baby? Hmm?" Then she weirdly turns and crouches down under me. She closes her eyes and places her palms close to my belly.

"*Back away from her!*" warns Bryce.

"It's okay, Bryce."

"It's not okay," Bryce snaps. "Don't let her touch you. It looks like she's casting. I warn you. Don't touch her! She's evil."

"What is evil?" Melanie asks. "Hmm? Am I evil?" She waves her fingers over my belly. Then she cackles again. "Surely you know there is great power in oomancy, warlock. Great power. Scramble the eggs and I'd have magnificent divination."

"*Stay the hell away from her!*" shouts Bryce.

Melanie bursts into laughter. Then she stands up and runs her fingers over his cheek. Bryce freezes like Enora.

"No, Bryce!" cries Maddie.

"Stop it, Melanie," I say. "Yes, I came to help Enora, but I also came to help you."

"Stop it, Melanie," Melanie hollers in my face. "Stop doing that! They're trying to help you!"

"She's insane, Cadence," cries Maddie. "Let's get the hell out of here."

"Maddie, no!"

Melanie flicks her wrist in Maddie's direction as if she's a bother. Maddie becomes immobile.

"Alondra couldn't come here to help you, Melanie," I say. "You'd never listen. But I'm here to try to take you away from this horrible place now."

"Such a handsome man you bring me," Melanie says, examining Bryce's face again. "Nice eyes. Nice smell. I bet, if not afraid, this man is very pretty. Strong arms. Strong legs. Did you bring this pretty and attractive man for me?"

"Will you return with me to Hawthorne?"

"No."

"Will you allow us to rid this field of devils then?"

"No."

"But these demons are not your friends. They hurt you."

"They obey you and me," she says, still examining Bryce's face. "Yes?"

"This has to end, Melanie. Enora will kill you if you disturb her coven."

"*Then I will kill her!*" she shouts in her beastly voice. "Didn't you learn that darkness guides you? What does it say now? Give the great and powerful Samhain Witch *gnosis*." She laughs. "Whisper me the occult, like your great teacher did last night. What will my shadows do for you if I dare hurt your friend? Or your husband? Or, by god, your baby? Hmm? What will you do with this newfound power, Cadence?"

"I'll protect them. These shadows are under my power now, and they will hurt you if you dare touch Bryce, Maddie, or my baby."

"*Yes!*" she croaks with a laugh. "*Yes, very good, Hassy!* Indeed. See, so you need shadows just like I do. Why would I want to leave them? They protect me too. Everyone wants to hurt us. If I cross you, you kill me. If I dare hurt this lovely man, or your unborn child, you kill me. You come all the way here to save me, but if I cross you, you send shadows to take my life. Do you now share in my confusion? You came to save me? Who on God's Earth will save you?"

Those white eyes stare right into mine. Then she breaks her gaze and shuffles over to Enora.

"Befuddled, confused witch. I made you speak evil. Then you repay me by joining this beastly witch to hurt me? Or *save* me?" she laughs, shaking her head. "Do you even know? But you did save me once. Why? To save yourself. Not for me. Not because we're *friends*. Not because you care about me. Just as you come here now. You don't come as a friend. Just like that mean, mean witch Enora tells you. She's no one's friend. You come here to make peace in Hawthorne for your husband and unborn child. You don't care about me. You just used my devils to stop your enemies." She cackles again. "And now, you admit you'd use them again to protect you. Or kill me. Confused, befuddled little girl."

"We never meant you harm."

"But you did! Just as their fucking witch council did! So did every witch that ever lived! And I promise you, I swear, that I will do everything to hurt the witches back!"

Then she starts weirdly banging her head with her hand.

"I...hate you! I hate all witches. I... I... I.... I give you thirty minutes to get out. I don't have a watch, but I still retain time in my hallowed mind. You have thirty minutes to get the hell out of my house. If you all do not leave, things will not end well for you. My mercy will end. Then I will use all the magic in *my family* to kill every single one of you. All your nice, nice friends. And then you. It has been the goal of my life to kill witches. You came here to *save* me? You just handed me every offender, stupid fool! But, behold... I am merciful. I give gnosis. Just like your conceited teacher. I teach you what Melanie has seen since she was a little girl. Melanie teaches you what Melanie sees. Now that you see, *fucking leave!* Till Samhain. But, then...come Samhain... I might just come and visit *my friends* in Hawthorne again... By the way, congratulations on your baby girl."

And she turns around and walks back toward the woods.

Bryce, Maddie, and Enora snap out of it. But the three of them seem so drowsy, as if in a daze. I hear murmuring behind me. A whole group of people in black robes are walking over from the parking lot. Was Melanie stopping them before? My friends are safe, but I've failed. In a few more steps, Melanie will disappear into the wilderness.

"I'm sorry, Melanie."

Melanie freezes before entering the woods, as if caught for a moment in the same freezing spell as Enora, Maddie, and Bryce. Then her whole body shakes. Because that voice wasn't mine, it was Alondra's.

"What did you say?" She slowly cocks her head back. "What did you just say to me?"

All the Ekimmu surrounding the glade rush up into the sky with their bodies flapping and waving in the wind. Then my approaching coven freezes. The dark shades circle Melanie and then fall behind her.

"You're sorry?" she asks, banging her head with her palm again. "Sorry? Sorry for what? For failing to help my family when they were haunted? For cursing our home and ruining us with your evil magic spells? Or are you sorry for sending your husband to bring my house down on my sister?"

There's no time to respond. I can't breathe. It's dark and my eyes are closed... She must have rushed at me, she is now choking my neck. I force myself to open an eye. Those white eyes, surrounded by filth and leafy muck, are staring down into mine.

"*Is that infernal witch inside you!*" asks Melanie. "*If Alondra hasn't left, I know a way to get her out! I can help you! I'll kill her vessel!*"

"I tried to remove the Ekimmu from this field," Alondra says with my lips. I don't know how, as I can barely breathe. "I failed. I'm sorry, Melanie."

"*Shut up!*"

Bryce tries to pry Melanie's fingers from my neck. So does Maddie. But Melanie's grip is too strong.

"*Get off her!*" cries Maddie.

"*Let her go!*" shouts Bryce.

Enora rushes over and tries to pry Melanie off me too. All three of them are trying to keep those sharp fingernails from cutting my skin and her fingers from squeezing my throat. From cutting off...my air. Her long, deformed fingernails stab at me. And...

"You failed, Allie! Just like you failed to keep them away from your coven! Taught more magic and spells to this ewe? Thought ewe would make things better? Where's my momma! Where's Winnie? Where's Daddy! You didn't help anyone. You cursed, poisoned, and killed everyone!"

"Get off of her!" cries Maddie again.

I can't... I can't breathe!

"Would you have accepted my apology if I had come before I died?" Alondra somehow asks from my lips. She sounds so calm as I gasp for air.

"I would have killed you!" Melanie shouts in my face. I close my eyes again as she squeezes me tighter than ever. *"I will kill you now, like I intend to kill every witch left in this world!"*

"Stop it," cries Bryce. *"My god, stop choking her!"*

"Get off her!" cries Maddie again.

"The demons destroyed you, Melanie," Alondra says, strangely calm. "It is my fault. And the witch's council. Liam and Kenosha. So many of us have hurt you. But now you hunt us? You are the most wicked witch in the world. If you are bent on hunting every witch, you must kill yourself. Heed Alondra's final warning: Yes, you may destroy me. But this light, the only light I had left before I died, was brought down to try to help you. Kill your sister, Cadence, and I will go, but all will come to ruin for you. You will bring an imbalance, rage and sorrow, so dark that it will surely not only destroy me and Cadence but destroy Hawthorne and everything left of you."

"Vade retro, daemon!" cries Bryce. He holds aloft *Broomstick.* *"Vade retro! Get off her!"*

Melanie's head is struck by an invisible force, as if by a club. But her fingers still clasp my neck.

"Leave this child," Escoba's voice says, struggling to speak through my lips. *"Cast Jumbee under the cross and grace of God."*

"*How many fucking witches are inside there!*" Melanie shouts.

"*I call upon the shining light of Venus!*" cries Enora. She is trying so hard to pry Melanie's hands off me too. "*Off her, daemon! Off Windstorm! Get off! Lux tenebris. By the light of Lucifer, release this body. I command you. Satanas. Satanas. Upon my power, vade retro! Vade retro!*"

Melanie's head is struck again, this time with enough force to finally throw her from me. But Enora, Bryce, and Maddie are thrown too.

Enora quickly shuffles along the ground, searching the grass. She grabs her wand. Then she rises on a knee and points it at Melanie. All the demons move behind Enora.

Melanie just smiles. Her disgusting grin alone seems to force Enora to drop the wand.

"*Vade prae,*" Melanie says quietly with a smirk. "*Vade prae.* The demons are under my control and Cassie-Hassyhorn's now, not yours, you bad bad Abaddon witch."

Enora's whole body is thrown forward, sliding along the grass, stopping at Melanie's left hand. Then my body is thrown back, and I'm hauled to her right hand. And then...

God, I feel that horrible squeeze again...no, the choking...

"*Get off her! Please! Stop!*" cries Bryce. He holds *Broomstick* aloft again. "*Vade retro! Vade retro!*"

An invisible force strikes Melanie's face over and over, but it isn't enough to stop her from choking Enora and me.

"Please...Melanie," I say with my own voice. "Please. Stop it!"

"*Prae daemon?*" Melanie asks. "*Prae?*"

Cadence. Daughter. Melanie killed her mother. She called you Kathy. Do you think she wanted to kill her mother?

"One final lesson, witches, before you both die!" shouts Melanie. Her wicked eyes, now not only bright from the surrounding filth, but *all* white due to her magic. "Life does not last long after air leaves the chest. Then goes the heart. And then, evil ewe, what shall happen to your sweet unborn child? That little baby growing inside of you?"

"I'm sorry, Melanie," I say, but it's not Alondra. This time it's Melanie's mom, Kathy. "Will you ever forgive me? I'm so sorry for everything that happened to us. To Winnie. To pa. I'm so sorry for everything that went wrong in this cursed place. I never meant for your life to be so hard. I will never blame you for what you did to me and pa. I forgive you, my darling. I forgive you. We love you. But I wonder...will you ever forgive me?"

22

FORGIVE ME

It's dark. The cuts on my neck burn. My throat stings. It's so dark and so cold. Am I dead? God, what about Chandra? No. Please, God, please just save my baby girl. I don't care anything about myself, but please save Chandra and Bryce. Please. They mean everything to me. Take my life, if you must, but please save them. Please, God, save my family and forgive me.

I see light. Light shines forth, the brightest light I've ever seen.

23

FORGIVE HER

I OPEN MY EYES, LYING ON MY SIDE GASPING FOR AIR. THEN I cough, trying hard to breathe. My neck hurts so bad. And then...I hear crying. At first, I think it sounds like a baby. Chandra? How? She's not even born yet. No, it's...Melanie.

Melanie is lying on her side not far from me, clutching her stomach, sobbing. The demons have left us and, with their darkness gone, I squint at the bright yellow-white rays of the sun above us. Enora isn't far from me. She meets my gaze, but she's not getting up. She seems too weak—she's coughing and struggling to breathe too. *Was she trying to save me?* Bryce and Maddie are kneeling next to me. And behind them, I see our friends running toward us. I think Melanie's magic had kept them back again. Well, she's not stopping them now. Melanie's too busy crying.

I struggle to get up, but I feel too weak. Maddie and Bryce hold me.

"Oh, Cadence, are you all right?" Bryce asks.

"Just take it slow, babe," Maddie says.

I nod. But then I point at Melanie. "Help her." Thankfully it's my own voice. "Please. Not me...just help her."

"*God, Momma!*" Melanie shouts, in tears. "*God, I'm so sorry! God, what have I done! What did I do to you and Papa! Forgive me. Please. Will you ever forgive me!*"

Kenosha rushes to me. Then comes Frida, Maddie, Jane, and Liam. Everyone in my coven is rushing around me. I cough again, trying to take in breaths. My throat still stings. They try to help me up, but I'm staring at Melanie. Weirdly, the witch's mud is gone. She's dirty, but not covered in black tarry mud. She's also not bald. She has long golden-blond hair, like Jane's. Her features are clearer. She's not that much older than I am. And her long blond hair reminds me of Jane—like a younger Aunt Jane.

It's Jane who helps her sit up. But Melanie's inconsolable.

"I'm Jane," Aunt Jane says pointing to her chest.

Melanie looks up and sees Liam. She ignores even him. She looks too sad, so sad that I want to cry with her.

Enora walks away without a word. No one pays any attention. Can you blame us? I'm guessing she's heading back to her coven.

Frida hugs me so tightly.

"What can we do for her, Mom?" Maddie asks Aunt Jane, looking at Melanie.

"Forgive her," Frida says.

I gaze over Frida's shoulder at the grassy field. The demons are still here. Now, under such a bright sun, they truly are shadows. They will always be here. So many more cower in the woods surrounding the fields like black statues. They are twisting and turning, soiling the ground, polluting the beauty of the forest with their disgusting stench of decay. They are far darker and more repulsive than the Samhain Witch. But, though these Ekimmu may never leave the glade, I believe that, finally, the Samhain Witch is gone.

24

BLESSED BE

I'M TAKING A BREATHER FROM THE WEDDING RECEPTION, LEANING against a wooden column on my outdoor patio, staring out at the wild grass in the yard. The backyard's packed with bodies wearing suits and formal dresses. I'm still wearing my long violet bridesmaid dress. And the bride—Mom?—she's still in her lovely white dress.

Aunt Jane is dancing with Dad in the center of my glade by the bonfire logs. I have to admit, they look cute together. We've got some mellow eighties music Aunt Jane likes, playing through the speakers beside me. And you know those violet flames—the ones I've seen every day around the logs since last year? They are finally gone.

Maddie and Tammy are standing by a table yapping. So are many other witches of my coven. Little Sophie, still in her adorable white dress, is playing tag with her new boyfriend, my seven-year-old cousin Kyle. And Frida and Tammy are sitting at a table with their fiancés eating cake.

"Cadence," says a male voice behind me. "Congratulations."

It's Liam. I tip my shades down and do the best I can to smile back.

"You leaving?" I ask.

"Already extended the trip a week under the circumstances. Yeah, we have to get back. I have to get back to work. How are you holding up?"

"Better than her," I say, gesturing to a pale woman sitting alone quietly in a white plastic chair. She has long blond hair and is wearing a short lime-green dress—Aunt Jane's dress. It's Melanie. Like me, she's just quietly watching everybody.

"You saved her," Liam says.

"She's completely lost." I shake my head and sigh. "Aunt Jane and Maddie are doing everything they can, but half the time she just talks to herself. The only good thing is, she's not mean. She just smiles. Maybe she's as averse to spellcasting as you now?"

"Hope so. I think she'll get better with medication. We just need to give it time."

"Is that your assessment as a psychologist or a warlock?"

"Psychologist. Allie was my wife, remember? I gladly gave up the magic business a long time ago."

"Aha," I say with a laugh. "Well, madness could have been my fate. Melanie is the most powerful witch there ever was. She sees the same demons I can, but I'm not sure she can turn it off. All this necromancy messed up her mind. It's funny because she hunted us, but now, I suppose, she hunts herself."

"Alondra once told me that every witch risks madness when learning the dark arts."

"I never wanted to learn it."

"Neither did I, Cadence. But I don't think you could have helped her without it."

"Okay," I say with a nod. "Sure."

Then I look back at the wedding party. He clams up too, putting his hands in his pockets uncomfortably. We're often uncomfortable around each other, I guess.

"You still hate me?" he asks.

"Aha, pretty much," I say with a fake grin. But then I realize he came over to say goodbye, so I extend my arms for a hug. "Bye, Liam. No, I don't hate you, just like I don't hate Alondra. But I'll never accept the past. Thanks for coming to Dad's wedding."

Bryce walks outside.

"Leaving, man?" Bryce asks Liam, touching his shoulder.

Liam looks down at my belly and smiles. "Until she arrives. Then I'll be back to see my granddaughter."

"Well, don't go yet," Bryce says, gesturing to the sliding glass door. "Another guest just arrived."

"Why, is that Liam Johansen?" asks a boisterous voice with a thick southern accent. "Well, I'll be. And Cadence here too."

"Hi, Uncle Hanley," Liam says.

"Hi, Uncle Hanley," I echo.

"Don't you two 'hi' me. Come over and give pops a hug! Both of ya."

And we embrace him.

"You nearly missed us," Liam says. "We're leaving."

"So soon?" Uncle Hanley asks. "Not till you catch me up. How's Pamela? Sophie?"

And they keep talking.

I lean back on my column and glance at our guests again. Melanie's not looking at them anymore. She's staring into the woods. She's so weird. Following her gaze, there's nothing out there but the shadows of trees surrounding the yard.

"Abaddon!" Melanie cries, jumping up and opening her eyes wide. Then she bursts into laughter. "Abaddon. Abaddon." It's like someone told her the funniest joke ever. Like I said, weird.

She points like crazy at our trees.

I gaze in the direction she's pointing. It's just our woods surrounding my backyard...no...wait a minute...there is something there.

A figure in a black cloak with a hood over her head is walking toward us. It's Alondra! She's transparent, but as real as if she had gone missing and decided to return home.

"Bryce," I snap, whirling around. "Bryce!" But Bryce is already staring.

"At least she's not inside you," he mutters with a nod.

"You really see her?"

Bryce nods.

So many of my sisters are staring. Mira and Courtney were just eating cake on paper plates and chatting with Abella. Now they're rushing over, pointing, and showing Mandy, Gilda, and Helen. But, I think, so many others from the wedding party still don't see her.

"Well, I'm so sorry I couldn't make the ceremony," Uncle Hanley says. "I had an emergency to attend to on the farm. I tell you, your father couldn't be getting married to a nicer gal, Cadence. I'm just glad Liam didn't slip out before I could say hi. Why, and there's his girl. And what a perfect day for it all, Cadence. I've always loved this yard, you know. Despite all the witching going on, this backyard is lovelier than anything back on the farm."

Melanie is crouched over, now guffawing like a complete raving lunatic. I mean she is one, only she's not hallucinating. Unless Bryce and I are hallucinating too.

"Abaddon!" Melanie cries in laughter. "Abaddon!"

Liam's staring too.

Mira and a whole group of others slowly walk toward the vision. Maddie grabs my brother and glances at me. I nod. But, as everybody else heads to the trees, Pamela walks back to the house, holding little Sophie's hand, totally oblivious like Uncle Hanley.

"Ready to go, Lee?"

He sure isn't.

Uncle Hanley furrows his brow, finally noticing the crowd

forming. It must seem so weird for those who don't see the ghost.

"One second, Pam," Liam says. "There's one more guest I want to say goodbye to before we go."

Liam, Bryce, and I walk together toward the apparition. We're closest. Frida and Tammy and their fiancés, Greg and Nate, are walking over too. And Debra, Josie, Abella, and Gilda are heading cautiously over. Following us, not far behind, is half the wedding party.

We stop when Alondra removes her hood. Her penetrating emerald eyes shine like the white eyes of the Ekimmu, but they're as real as the lush green leaves surrounding her. And yet, this is not Alondra, my professor, this is Allie back when she was my age.

"The greatest regret in my life is that we never said goodbye," Alondra says to Liam. "I asked Cadence to bring you back to Hawthorne. Take it as..." And she actually smirks. "A bit of Luciferian pride. I wanted you to be here for me. Not for Hawthorne, but for me, Lee. For I could not be here now without you. Because, you see, outside of magic, there never was anything else to define me other than you."

Liam just nods, wiping his eyes.

"Goodbye, my love," Allie says with a nod.

And then they embrace. By magic, or through the power of her ghostly spirit, whatever the case, the two of them actually embrace as if Alondra were really here.

"We were right about her, Allie," Liam says, slowly backing up. He cocks his head back at me. "My vision of her was right. Cadence is our hope. She's the one who saved Hawthorne."

"Is it really her?" I ask.

"I think it's because of your magic," Liam says brushing tears from his eyes. "Or the energy of these grounds. It's our home, Cadence." Liam tears his eyes away from Alondra. "She's really here," he says with a nod. "Say goodbye, Cadence."

"I already did," I say flippantly.

"Katie," chides Bryce.

But Alondra actually laughs.

A large party is now standing behind me. I hear them more than see them. They're keeping their distance but murmuring like crazy. Some of the non-witches don't believe my sisters, I hear. But I catch one guest, old Aunt Mable, showing everybody pictures on her cellphone. And Melanie has gone from catatonic to complete manic-nutso, laughing and repeatedly uttering, "*Abaddon, Abaddon.*"

When I turn back to Alondra, her face has changed. She appears older. This is the Alondra I knew as my professor and mentor.

"Goodbye, Cadence. Goodbye, Bryce."

"Goodbye, Alondra," I say. I feel a tear fall from my eye too.

"Behold the maiden transformed into a mother," Alondra says to me. "Behold the Hawthorne Witch. Blessed be and may you never thirst, Cadence Wallace."

"Is that all you have to say? Cold witchy clichés? I kind of liked your words to Liam better."

"I see," she says, pensively nodding. "Then...how 'bout this...in the beginning there was darkness. And upon darkness, God said, let there be light. God *said*, Cadence. All *words* are creation. *Words* mean everything. Even a bunch of cold witchy platitudes. Is that better?"

"I really hate you."

Liam and Bryce laugh.

Alondra nods solemnly and turns to Liam. Despite the tears in his eyes, he has a smirk, probably amused by my endless feud with her.

"The woman you saw in our yard by the bonfire, Liam," Alondra says, "the one you predicted to save Hawthorne, that was not Cadence. It was our unborn granddaughter. Because, you see, Cadence does not believe her own eyes. I would never pass my magic and coven to such an infernal, stubborn nonbeliever."

Liam laughs more, still wiping tears from his eyes.

Bryce gently takes my hand in his. I squeeze it tightly.

"Bryce," Alondra says with a nod. "Cadence. Congratulations."

"For our baby?" Bryce asks.

"No," she says, "for your marriage. You two have always been wonderful together."

He hugs me and kisses my cheek again. I feel one of his tears falling on my cheek.

"Goodbye, Alondra," I say. "We all love you."

"And I love you, Cadence." She nods slowly. Then she looks over my shoulder. "I love all the witches in my circle in Hawthorne. Goodbye Bryce. Goodbye Kenosha. Madison. Tammy. Mira. Frida. Goodbye...Jane. Owl Jay."

"Oh, Allie," Jane says.

"Blessed be, Jane." Then Alondra addresses everyone. "Behold the two-faced goddess and the green man. Cadence and Bryce Wallace. Now Jane and Richard Hawthorne. Ouroboros. Hawthorne Witch, you tread now where I could not go. But, alas, as I leave, I wonder...will you miss me when I'm gone?"

Then, as she gazes at all of us, she slowly fades away.

I turn to Liam. He looks so sad.

"I'm sorry, Liam."

"We regret so many things from our past," he says with a nod.

Then I turn and face all the people in the wedding party, now standing behind us. Kenosha's joined the crowd, but in a lovely long black dress and curly wig. Even Melanie finally rose from her chair and is walking over. Even Dad, though I have a feeling he didn't see her and doesn't get what's going on. Back by the patio, Uncle Hanley and a few other onlookers look completely bewildered.

Bryce looks so sad that it makes me put my arms around him, reach up on my tippy toes, and kiss him on the lips.

"I love you, Cadence Wallace," he says. Then he rubs my belly. And that makes me kiss him more. But then I realize everybody's watching us.

"Guys, come on, let's get back to the party," I say. "Enjoy some cake. Wine. Enjoy our company. Jeesh, what's the matter with all of you? Never saw a witch in Hawthorne before?"

THE END

WITCHY ADVENTURES ARE CONTINUED IN THE HOLIDAY SHORT STORY, CANDY CRONE, IN THE HAWTHORNE UNIVERSITY WITCH SERIES

THE SERIES

- BROOMSTICK
- WINDSTORM
- THE HAWTHORNE WITCH
- WITCH MIRROR
- RAVENS
- SHADOW CAST
- BELTANE FIRE short story prequel
- SAMHAIN WITCH short story (3.5)
- CANDY CRONE (6.5)
- ALONDRA 20 yr prequel

THE BOXED SETS

- THE HAWTHORNE UNIVERSITY WITCH SERIES
- THE HAWTHORNE UNIVERSITY WITCH SERIES (4-6)
- THE HAWTHORNE UNIVERSITY WITCH HOLIDAY COLLECTION

AND DON'T FORGET THAT THE ENTIRE SERIES IS NOW AVAILABLE ON AUDIO, PERFORMED BY ALEXA ELMY AND PRESTON GEER!

ALSO BY A.L. HAWKE

PARANORMAL ROMANCE

- THE HAWTHORNE UNIVERSITY WITCH SERIES I-III
- THE HAWTHORNE UNIVERSITY WITCH SERIES 4-6
- THE HAWTHORNE UNIVERSITY WITCH HOLIDAY COLLECTION

- SHADES
- HAUNTING JOY
- PHANTOM MASQUERADE

- MY EVIL EYE
- THE GUARDIAN
- NECTAR OF AMBROSIA
- CORA

FANTASY: THE AZURE SERIES

- HARMONIA
- CORA: RISE OF THE FALLEN GODDESS
- AZURE BLUE
- CORAL RED
- PRINCESS SOJOURN

SCIENCE FICTION

- CANDY SAVANT SERIES

Books available at https://alhawke.com/books

PARTING WORDS

What did you think of *Shadow Cast*? By placing a book review, you can inform others of your thoughts and help spread the word about my book.

Want more? Periodically I like to send news regarding current or new projects. If you'd like to be privy, I encourage you to sign up to my email newsletter. Your information will remain private and you can cancel any time.

Sign up at www.alhawke.com or scan the following QR code:

AFTERWORD

I could never have imagined how important Cadence's story would become in my life when I first dreamt of her many years back. The original first few chapters were, quite honestly, dry. I threw the original manuscript in the trash. But that's because it was written with a different main character. The novel took on a life of its own when I introduced Cadence Hawthorne. This series has since been a journey for both Cadence and I.

Broomstick, my first witch book, was set to just be a Halloween novel. Seriously. The covid pandemic had emerged, the world had been turned on its head, and I was writing at a time when I still wasn't even sure whether I wanted to write science fiction or fantasy. I think the fact that my mother had passed at a time long enough for me to finally feel comfortable sharing my personal bereavement led Cadence to come to life in my first book. *Windstorm* is my absolute favorite. This second novel balances sexual tension between Cadence and Bryce, good vs. evil, and magic vs. the mundane. It also introduces Cadence's archenemy, Enora. *Hawthorne Witch* completed the original trilogy *in college*. Cadence fights with her best friend and her brother, and, of course, Enora, but it finishes in a happy ending with Cadence and Bryce getting married.

I had thought this would be it. In the time between these books, I wrote a prequel through Liam's eyes, *Alondra*. I also created a short prequel for Cadence's Freshman year, *Beltane Fire*.

But it was last year, after I decided to transform the books into audio, that I decided to write a new trilogy. Alexa Elmy, my narrator, did such an amazing job that she spurred my interest in writing about Cadence again. It had been her performance of Alondra that made me select her for the voice of my audiobook. Now I wanted to bring Alondra back. I had already written a split-personality novel, *My Evil Eye*, with Medusa talking to herself. So I thought of how much fun and exciting a novel would be, with audio featuring Alexa Elmy, if Alondra pops up *inside* Cadence's head as a ghost possession. *Witch Mirror* was born. In the subsequent books, and the short story *Samhain Witch* in between, I went back to researching and studying the occult. I had a background in religious studies back in college, which helped my understanding, but it wasn't until I researched this new series that I really got into real "magick". *Ravens*, the second in my second "trilogy", like *Windstorm* before it, is another one of my personal favorites. The simplicity of *Ravens* and the whole "anti-Cadence"-thing going on with this novel makes it stand out. There's tons of action and mystery. And there's a side of Cadence that hadn't shown through before. Her *evil* side. Finishing up my new trilogy was *Shadow Cast*. Ah, last but not least. The two hardest novels I've ever written have been *Mother Savant* and *Shadow Cast*. Why? Both books wrap up a series. An ending of a series, like the ending of a book, is always a struggle because they give the very significant problem of meaning. *Shadow Cast* went through a painful editing shuffling system. I literally shuffled the beginning chapters around to enhance flow. But it was worth it in the end. I'm satisfied with the final product as a conclusion to the series.

There never was going to be a "graduate" witch series (books 4-6). Well, after two short stories and a prequel, and, now, nine books total, you could say I've grown pretty fond of Hawthorne's magic and Cadence Hawthorne. And I think I succeeded in moving Cadence from maiden to mother (the triple goddess Celtic phases of life).

Will there be a final trilogy from mother to krone? Who knows? But I kinda feel bad for Cadence, in a way. It seems I keep putting her through so much pain and hardship.

Thanks to all of you for loving Cadence Hawthorne and all her friends as much as I do. Thanks for taking this fun journey with me!

Blessed be, readers. And may you never thirst (or end).

A.L. Hawke

ACKNOWLEDGMENTS

I want to thank Stephanie Marshall Ward. The first book she ever edited was book I of the series, *Broomstick*. She's line edited every other book written by me since (what does that tell you?). And thank you to Alexa B. for proofreading all my pesky grammatical errors. She is also my go-to editor for my books. Thanks, once again, to George B. for beta reading *all* the witchy books in my series. Thank you to Alexa Elmy for converting every book in my series into audio and being the voice of Cadence and Alondra (and the rest of the gang). And last, but hardly least, thank you, Brosedeignz, for understanding my vision and creating amazing covers (books 3.5-6.5). Every one of you has shaped this series. THANK YOU!

ABOUT THE AUTHOR

A.L. Hawke is the author of the bestselling Hawthorne University Witch series. The author lives in Southern California torching the midnight candle over lovers against a backdrop of machines, nymphs, magic, spice and mayhem. A.L. Hawke writes fantasy and romance spanning four thousand years, from pre-civilization to contemporary and beyond.

Visit A.L. Hawke at www.alhawke.com

Email: contact@alhawke.com

www.ingramcontent.com/pod-product-compliance
Lightning Source LLC
Chambersburg PA
CBHW032221190726
48289CB00007BA/2327